THE RATTENBURY MYSTERY

When the infamous theatrical agent Amos Rattenbury is found stabbed to death in his London office, the weight of suspicion falls on Dorene Grey, a young actress. Assistant Commissioner, Sir Digby Hilton of Scotland Yard, is assigned to find the missing Dorene. However, she has two champions: Sir Digby's brother Terry, and the mysterious figure known as 'The Phantom of the Films'. And she will need their help to escape the fate planned for her by a cunning murderer.

Books by John Russell Fearn
in the Linford Mystery Library:

THE TATTOO MURDERS
VISION SINISTER
THE SILVERED CAGE
WITHIN THAT ROOM!
REFLECTED GLORY
THE CRIMSON RAMBLER
SHATTERING GLASS
THE MAN WHO WAS NOT
ROBBERY WITHOUT VIOLENCE
DEADLINE
ACCOUNT SETTLED
STRANGER IN OUR MIDST
WHAT HAPPENED TO HAMMOND?
THE GLOWING MAN
FRAMED IN GUILT
FLASHPOINT
THE MASTER MUST DIE
DEATH IN SILHOUETTE
THE LONELY ASTRONOMER
THY ARM ALONE
MAN IN DUPLICATE

JOHN RUSSELL FEARN

THE RATTENBURY MYSTERY

Complete and Unabridged

LINFORD
Leicester

First published in Great Britain

First Linford Edition
published 2007

British Library CIP Data

Fearn, John Russell, *1908 –1960*
    The Rattenbury mystery.—Large print ed.—
Linford mystery library
    1. Murder—Investigation—England—
London—Fiction 2. Missing persons—
Investigation—England—London—Fiction
    3. Detective and mystery stories
    4. Large type books
    I. Title
    823.9'12 [F]

ISBN 978–1–84617–982–2

Published by
F. A. Thorpe (Publishing)
Anstey, Leicestershire

Set by Words & Graphics Ltd.
Anstey, Leicestershire
Printed and bound in Great Britain by
T. J. International Ltd., Padstow, Cornwall

This book is printed on acid-free paper

1

'Very well, Miss Grey. You can consider yourself engaged on those terms,' said the agent. 'The contract will be ready for your signature at five o'clock. Good afternoon.'

Dorene Grey's step was light as she hurried through the shabby waiting room and descended the staircase to the busy London street. Her smooth girlish face was flushed, her eyes alight with pleased excitement as she passed through the swing doors which she had entered with such shrinking timidity less than half an hour since.

But those thirty minutes had changed her whole outlook on life. The thing that had then seemed so hopeless of fulfilment was now an accomplished fact. The dream of her life had come true!

Her smile became even more radiant as she recalled how she had hesitated, half minded to turn back without entering the

office at all. She had felt that her journey to London was nothing but a waste of money; that it was sheer madness for an inexperienced girl to hope to get an engagement in a film studio; that she was a conceited little fool to have taken any notice of the advertisement. And when at last she had plucked up courage to enter, she had steeled herself beforehand to meet with failure.

But all her misgivings had proved groundless. Instead of being met with the expected rebuff her timid enquiry had been received with polite attention. The extremely stout old gentleman had actually seemed pleased to see her. He had smiled genially while she had answered the few questions that he had put to her. Then — wonder of wonders! — he had casually offered her a small part in a forthcoming film.

Even now she could scarcely believe that her dream had so quickly crystallized into actual fact; that the contract — her first contract — the magic key that might unlock the gates leading to fame and fortune — was to be ready for her to sign

at five o'clock that afternoon; that her entry into the charmed world of Filmdom was practically accomplished.

Immersed in her pleasant daydreams, Dorene Grey had reached the busy junction of traffic where Oxford Street intersects Charing Cross Road. Pausing for a moment for a chance of crossing the crowded road, her eyes encountered the posters displayed outside the cinema on the corner. A little smile curved her red lips as she reflected that at no distant date these same boards might blazon her own name, her own picture, to an admiring world. Behind the flaunting lettering there seemed to stretch a golden path, leading to the shining Temple of Fame with its doors wide open to welcome her in.

'Pardon me,' said a quiet voice at her elbow.

Dorene's train of thought snapped as she turned and saw a man by her side in the act of raising his hat. Abruptly she turned away, a flush of vexation and embarrassment deepening the colour of her cheeks. But by that fleeting glimpse

she saw that he was young, well-built and handsome — too handsome to be trusted, she decided swiftly.

Without troubling to reply she started to cross the road, but the stranger laid his hand upon her arm with a courteous yet compelling gesture.

'You are quite right to be annoyed, Miss Grey,' he said in a cultivated voice. 'I hate to accost you in the street, but there is something that I must say to you. Am I wrong in assuming that you have just been offered an engagement by Amos Rattenbury?'

Sheer surprise prevented the girl from returning any other answer than a silent nod.

'You will be well advised to forego that engagement Miss Grey,' the stranger said calmly.

'Why?' Dorene demanded, angry rebellion flaming in her eyes.

'For many reasons,' he answered, with an almost pitying glance at her fresh and innocent countenance. 'Believe me, I have not thrust myself into this matter without good cause.'

4

'Indeed?' she returned, in as frigid a tone as she could assume. 'Is that intended as the cue at which I register overwhelming gratitude?'

The man gave a boyish laugh and shook his head.

'It will meet the case if you register just a little commonsense,' he countered swiftly. 'But I can't say what I have to say right here on the pavement. I will not ask you to lunch somewhere with me, because I know that you'll refuse.' Then a smile of amusement lit up his handsome features. 'I have it!' he cried. 'The British Museum is just round the corner. Let's go and have our confab among the mummies. There you will breathe the very atmosphere of respectability and be under the eyes of the myrmidons of the law the whole time!'

There was something infectious about his manner that Dorene, while fully intending to meet his proposal with a freezing refusal, somehow or other found herself walking by his side up a quiet side street and presently ascending the steps of the great grime-crusted Grecian portico

and entering the glass doors of the museum.

It was nearing closing time, and the long, lofty galleries were almost deserted. Choosing a seat in the shadow of a huge granite statue of some forgotten Egyptian king, the strange young man abruptly checked the flow of trivial conversation which he had hitherto kept up, and his face became intensely serious as he took up the thread of their former talk.

'I'm going to put all my cards on the table, Miss Grey, and if you are wise you will do the same. In the first place, let me introduce myself. If you are interested in matters theatrical, my name may not be totally unknown to you. Does 'Terry Hilton' convey anything to your mind?'

'I seem to have heard the name before,' the girl confessed after a short pause.

He gave a slight shrug and his features twisted in a whimsical grimace.

'Such is fame!' he exclaimed with an air of mock tragedy. 'Young lady, my name has topped the bills from one end of the country to the other.'

'So you are an actor?' she cried.

Terry Hilton nodded gravely, sternly repressing an inclination to laugh.

'Yes, I think I can with justice describe myself as such. Heaven knows, I make the assertion in no boastful spirit. I merely mention the fact in order to convince you that I know what I'm talking about when I warn you to beware of Amos Rattenbury.'

'But why?' she asked, her eyes widening with genuine bewilderment. 'I thought that Mr. Rattenbury was most kind to offer me the engagement, and I'm certainly not going to throw away my chance without knowing the reason why.'

'You shall know the reason why in good time,' he answered quietly. 'But first I should like to know how you first got in touch with this fellow.'

'I happened to see an advertisement in our local paper.'

'Exactly,' he commented dryly. 'Asking for young ladies for film work, intimating that previous experience was not necessary, but, I dare swear, stipulating that applicants must be young, good-looking, and willing to travel abroad.'

'Why,' she cried in surprise. 'Did you see the advertisement?'

His face hardened as he shook his head. 'No,' he said grimly. 'But I know Rattenbury's methods.'

For a few moments Dorene quietly studied the actor's face. It was not merely good-looking; there was character and intelligence in the lofty brow, determination in the lines of the chin, kindly humour in the dark, expressive eyes. Dorene felt that he was speaking the truth and that his motives were disinterested. Yet it was hard to relinquish the prize that was already within her grasp, to throw away the chance of playing an important part at the very commencement of her career.

Terry Hilton seemed to sense her train of thought for he went on: 'A man who has a decent engagement to offer does not require to advertise in local country papers. There are thousands of actresses, young, talented and good-looking, seeking work — 'resting' is the polite term — at the present moment. But Rattenbury has no use for these girls. They know

too much about his rotten business. He's only out to snare innocent young simpletons who are dazzled at the prospect of becoming a shining star without having to fight their way up from the bottom by sheer hard work.'

It was not a very tactful speech, but Terry was too excited to pick and choose his words. The idea of that young and beautiful girl — a mere child so far as knowledge of the world was concerned — walking blindly and trustfully into the toils of a monster so unspeakably foul as he knew Amos Rattenbury to be, moved him to pity and indignation. But he did not realize how badly he had blundered until Dorene rose abruptly to her feet, her eyes hard with anger.

'Thank you for your very frank and unflattering estimate of my intelligence, Mr. Hilton, but I fail to see why I should allow myself to be dictated to by you. I am quite capable of managing my own affairs, and I intend to sign that contract.'

'When?' He asked the question so quickly that she found herself answering without thinking.

'At five o'clock this afternoon.'

He shrugged slightly and inclined his head with the air of one who accepts defeat.

'Then be sure to read it through carefully before putting your name to it.' He slipped his hand into his pocket, and when he withdrew it she caught the silvery glint of metal between his fingers.

'Here is a little friend in need,' he said, quickly thrusting the object into her hand. 'Don't be afraid to use it if you find yourself in danger.'

He raised his hat, turned on his heel abruptly, and strode away from the gallery until he turned a corner and was hidden from her sight. Only then did she glance at the thing she held in her hand.

It was a silver-plated whistle, some three inches in length, and on it were engraved the words, 'Metropolitan Police'.

2

There are some old stagers who proudly boast that they made their first appearance on the boards as the innocent 'che-e-ild' of some luckless heroine starving to death (to the accompaniment of slow music, blue limelight, and a paper snowstorm) on the doorstep of the heartless villain.

Terry Hilton, however, could make no such claim. His family was not even remotely connected with the stage. He came of a long line of distinguished soldiers, and his eldest brother, the present Sir Digby Hilton, had carried on the family tradition. After a distinguished career Sir Digby had been offered, and had accepted, the post of Assistant Commissioner of Police; and Terry, although he was looked upon as being the least successful member of the family from a monetary point of view, was a frequent and welcome visitor at his

brother's private office within the grim precincts of New Scotland Yard.

It was there that Terry made his way immediately after parting from Dorene Grey.

'I've come to you for a bit of advice and help, old man,' Terry opened the interview by remarking in a confidential tone.

'Always pleased to be of assistance,' Digby murmured mechanically. 'What's the trouble?'

Terry laughed and shook his head.

'Oh, it's not my trouble — I'm worrying myself with somebody else's troubles for a change!' Abruptly his face became serious as he went on: 'You've heard of Amos Rattenbury?'

'The agent fellow? I should say I have! I've had my official eye on his doings for some time.'

'I was at his office this afternoon.'

Sir Digby's brows shot up in amazement.

'What on earth induced you to visit a man like that?'

'Oh, it was just a fluke.' Terry Hilton leaned across the desk and helped himself

to a cigarette. 'I happened to be passing the door when I saw a girl, a rather decent looking kid, glance at the newspaper she held in her hand, hesitate a moment or two, and go in. Knowing the kind of swine that Rattenbury is, I nipped in after her. Luckily the waiting room was empty, so I had an opportunity of doing a bit of eavesdropping. I found out that her name was Dorene Grey, and that she had come up to London from a little village in Kent in answer to his advertisement. By means of a few skilful questions, Rattenbury led her on to talk about herself. She was the daughter of a doctor, who had recently died, leaving her practically alone in the world.'

Sir Digby was beginning to look rather bored.

'All this is very interesting, no doubt, but I fail to see where I come into it. Rattenbury is a crook, but he's mighty careful to keep within the letter of the law. This is a free country, and if a girl wants to sign a contract to act in the films we can't stop her. The most that we can do is to give her a friendly word of warning.'

'I have already done that — and got badly snubbed for my pains,' Terry said savagely.

'Quite so,' laughed the other man. 'There are three types of persons who are simply incapable of listening to reason — a person in love, a person in drink, and a person who is stage-struck. Experience is a dear school, but fools will learn in no other,' he quoted cynically. 'If you have anything definite on which to base a charge, I may be able to do something about the matter. Officially we know nothing whatever against the man, or he would not be holding a licence from the L.C.C., and I should be placing myself in a false position by interfering. You can't charge a man with intending to commit a crime unless he has been previously convicted of the same offence.'

'Then you refuse to move in this matter?'

'Produce your evidence and we'll move fast enough.' Sir Digby gave his brother a sharp look. 'You seem to be taking a very great interest in this young lady, my boy. One doesn't need to be the head of a

police department to deduce the fact that she is rather nice looking.'

'She has the face of an angel,' Terry cried enthusiastically.

'Really?' There was a hint of dryness in the police official's voice as he went on: 'Then has it not struck you that Rattenbury may possibly see his way to make a real star out of her? He is a shrewd businessman, and I suppose he has eyes in his head just the same as you have.'

Terry Hilton eyed his brother gloomily.

'You may be right, Digby,' he said after a long pause. 'I hope and pray that you *are* right. I am not an imaginative man, but something seems to warn me that that girl is in danger — great danger. She said that she was going back to Rattenbury's office at five o'clock, to sign the contract. I think I'll stroll round that way myself,' he added thoughtfully, 'my presence may be useful.'

Sir Digby uttered an unexpected laugh.

'You'll be a trifle late, my boy,' he said, shooting back his cuff and glancing at his wrist. 'It's twenty minutes past five now.'

'Good Lord!' exclaimed the young actor, starting to his feet. 'I've been forgetting how the time was going. Is it really so late? I shall have to rush.'

His brother gently forced him back into the chair he had just vacated.

'It would be far better if you just sit there quietly and smoke another cigarette while I sign these papers. Then you can come home with me and have a bit of dinner, and afterwards — '

The bell of the desk telephone tinkled, and Sir Digby broke off in the middle of the sentence and placed the receiver to his ear.

'Certainly — I'm going right now,' said Terry as, eager to be gone, he reached for his hat and made for the door. Before he could reach it, his brother's sharp exclamation caused him to halt.

'Hold on there, Terry!' The quiet tones sounded unusually strained. 'If you're going to Rattenbury's office I reckon I'll come along with you.'

Terry's face lit up with pleasure as he turned.

'You will?' he cried. 'That's real

sporting of you, Digby. But we must hustle.'

A bleak smile passed across the face of the Assistant Commissioner.

'We'll hustle all right!' he returned grimly. 'We're going to travel in a car belonging to the Flying Squad.'

'Flying Squad?' Terry repeated, obviously startled. 'Why have they been called out?'

Sir Digby Hilton replaced the receiver and jerked to his feet.

'They are about to drag London for the angel-faced girl in whom you take such an interest,' he said in crisp official tones. 'Amos Rattenbury has been murdered!'

3

The memory of the short, swift dash through the crowded London traffic lingered long in Terry Hilton's mind like the swift-moving scenes of some vivid nightmare. There were six men in the car besides Terry and Sir Digby, but scarcely a word was spoken after it had glided out beneath the frowning granite arch which guards the quadrangle of Scotland Yard. Each man seemed busy with his own thoughts, and Terry was glad enough of an opportunity of straightening out his own confused impressions.

In itself, the fact of Amos Rattenbury's sudden death gave him little concern. His name was a byword in the theatrical profession for everything that was vile, and the world would be all the sweeter for his removal. But he had been murdered — murdered at the very time when Dorene Grey had arranged to go to his office to sign the contract on which she

set such great hopes. It seemed the height of absurdity to connect her with such a crime. Yet, if she had kept the appointment, she must have been on the premises when the murder was committed. Terry's hands clenched involuntarily and his face grew hard as granite as his mind began dimly to sense a series of happenings that might well excuse any girl striking down such a man as Amos Rattenbury.

The time occupied by the journey seemed incredibly short, and when the car glided to a smooth standstill Terry could scarcely believe that they had covered the distance until he glanced out of the window.

The office of Rattenbury's Dramatic, Variety and Film Agency consisted of two moderate sized rooms on the first floor. The ground floor was occupied by a shop that sold sporting outfits, and was entirely cut off from the upper part of the building. A fairly spacious but dimly lighted staircase, leading from the main street, gave access to Rattenbury's office, and also to other offices on the

floors higher up.

There was a police constable lurking at the foot of the stairs, peering expectantly through the glass panels of the door. He came to attention and saluted as he recognized the Assistant Commissioner.

'How long have you been on duty here?' Sir Digby paused to ask.

'Since the tragedy was discovered, sir.'

'Nobody has left the building since then?'

'No, sir.'

'Very well. You had better come upstairs with us.' Sir Digby turned to one of the men who accompanied him. 'Inspector Renshaw, please detail a plain-clothes officer to take this man's place. His orders are to allow nobody to enter or leave while we are making our investigation.'

'Very good, sir.'

Terry Hilton followed in the rear of the little procession as they mounted the stairs. The waiting room was empty, but the sound of subdued voices came through the slightly open door leading to the private office.

'Certainly not more than an hour since,' said a crisp, businesslike voice. 'The body is still quite warm.'

Terry glanced at the clock on the mantlepiece, and noted that the hands were pointing to ten minutes to six. Fifty minutes ago Dorene Grey would have been having her interview with the murdered man!

The small room in which Terry Hilton found himself was overcrowded with furniture and decorated with a kind of tawdry magnificence. Any signs of taste or refinement were conspicuous by their total absence. The walls were covered with embossed paper on which tarnished gold flowers of unknown species straggled without visible means of support over a groundwork of silky green. Curtains of heavy crimson velvet hung at the windows. A carpet with inch-deep pile covered the floor, and scattered about on it were two oriental-looking settees and several deep armchairs. A very ornate desk, standing between the door and the fireplace, was the sole indication that the apartment was intended for business

purposes. The air was heavy with the cloying scent of some Eastern incense, which still rose in a thin, snakelike coil from a silver cup held aloft by statuettes of three slender nymphs.

Spread-eagled over one of the ottomans was the body of an immensely fat man. Even in life Amos Rattenbury had not been a particularly pleasant sight. Now, his appearance was such as to shake the stoutest nerves. But this was not due to the usual crimson sign-manuals which murder is apt to leave in its wake. Whatever traces of blood may have surrounded the silver dagger hilt which protruded from the left breast of his black waistcoat were rendered mercifully invisible by the colour of the cloth. It was the expression of frenzied fear and horror stamped on those leaden-hued features that made the corpse of Amos Rattenbury a thing to shudder at and to shun.

With a feeling very much akin to nausea, Terry turned away and devoted his attention to the living occupants of the room. A police-sergeant was busily

taking notes. A middle-aged man, obviously a doctor, had just finished examining the body. A shabbily dressed youth, pale and ill at ease, sat huddled up in one of the great armchairs.

The Assistant Commissioner, after one comprehensive glance round the room, turned and addressed the man in uniform.

'We'll have your report first, sergeant.'

'I was making my usual rounds, sir,' the man began in the toneless voice that every policeman seems instinctively to adopt when making official statements, 'and about 5.25 or thereabouts, I was talking to Police-constable Walker at the corner of Kingsway. There we were accosted by this man,' he indicated the youth with the pale face, 'who was in a highly excited state, and who informed us that his boss had been murdered in his office. I accompanied my informant to these premises, where I found the deceased lying in the position he now occupies. Then I rang up the Yard and the nearest doctor, whom I knew was Dr. Dugdale of Bloomsbury Square, just over

the road. He arrived within a few minutes, and at once pronounced life to be extinct, and he said — '

'All right, sergeant, thank you,' interposed Sir Digby. 'We'll have the medical report at first hand.' He glanced at the doctor, who nodded his agreement.

'The man was past medical aid when I arrived. Of course, it's impossible to say definitely before the post-mortem, but it's practically certain that the point of the weapon has penetrated the walls of the heart. In that case death would have been instantaneous.'

'In your opinion, could such a wound have been self-inflicted?'

Dr. Dugdale hesitated, glanced at the body, and then gave a dubious shrug.

'It's not physically impossible for a man to kill himself in such a manner,' he said guardedly.

The police sergeant stepped forward at this point.

'Beg pardon, sir. This man says that he heard the murdered man call out for help, and ring his bell as well.'

'Ah, that rules out suicide, at any rate.'

Digby turned to the man seated in the armchair. 'Now, then, my man, let's hear your story. First of all, what's your name?'

'Mifflin, sir — Albert Mifflin, and I live at Brewer's Buildings, Drury Lane. I am — was — Mr. Rattenbury's clerk, sir. I've been with him more'n a couple of years, and I've always given satisfaction. I didn't do him in, sir — I swear I didn't! It was that gal.'

Terry made a quick movement, but Sir Digby silenced him with a warning glance.

'Which girl?' By the tone of his question one would have thought that this was the first that the Assistant Commissioner had heard about there being a woman in the case.

'Why, the gal that visited Mr. Rattenbury this afternoon,' Albert Mifflin went on volubly. 'Miss Grey she called herself. Said she had an appointment with the boss — to sign a contract. I knocked on the door and showed her into his office — '

'What time was this?'

'Right on the stroke of five o'clock, sir.

25

I showed her in, closed the door, and went back to my desk in the waiting room. About a quarter of an hour or twenty minutes later I heard a noise in the boss's office.'

'What kind of a noise?'

'A scuffling noise,' Mifflin answered, after a long pause.

The police Commissioner glanced at him sharply. 'What did you do?'

'Nothing, sir.'

'Nothing?' There was an edge to Digby's voice as he repeated the word.

'No, sir.' Mifflin shuffled his feet and cleared his throat nervously. 'The boss didn't like to be disturbed while he was interviewing clients. I just took no notice, but when the bell rang I got up and tried the door. I couldn't open it, so I returned to my desk and went on with my work.'

'Was your master in the habit of locking the door while he interviewed his clients?'

The clerk shook his head.

'It doesn't need to be locked, sir. It closes with a spring catch when it is pulled to.'

Sir Digby Hilton strode to the door and glanced at the lock. 'H'm, a very unusual type of lock to be on an inner room,' he mused, fumbling with the handle. 'It seems to be out of order.'

'No, sir. It's quite all right,' said Mifflin, coming forward as though eager to display his knowledge. 'You press the handle inwards to pull back the catch. Like this — '

He gave a violent shove and the catch flew back. Sir Digby and the grey-haired police inspector exchanged a meaningful glance. It was obvious that anyone who did not know the secret method of manipulating the lock would be hopelessly trapped the moment the door was shut. Sir Digby, however, merely invited the man to continue his statement.

'Well as I was saying, sir, I went back to my desk, but no sooner had I sat down than I heard the boss shout 'Help!'. I went back to the door and called out, 'Is anything wrong, sir?'. There was no answer, so I repeated the question several times. Then I was sure that something was wrong, so I went again to my desk,

took out the passkey which I keep there, and opened the door. At first I thought the room was empty. Then I saw — that!' He jerked his thumb towards the motionless figure on the settee. 'The girl had disappeared.'

'She might have been hiding,' suggested Inspector Renshaw. 'Didn't it strike you to look behind these pieces of furniture?'

'No, it didn't,' Mifflin returned sulkily. 'If I'd gone poking round there by myself I might have been struck by something else besides an idea! I just took one look and then nipped out to call the police.'

'And is that all you know about the matter, Mifflin?' Digby went on.

'That's all, sir,' came the eager answer. 'It's the honest truth, sir, every word of it.'

'All right,' interrupted Sir Digby. 'Take him into the next room, inspector, and get his fingerprints.'

Mifflin gave a violent start, his eyes narrowed and a look of consternation swept over his bloodless face.

'Fingerprints!' he gasped. 'Anyone

would think that I'm a blinking crook! I'm an honest man, I am, and you can't put anything on me.'

Inspector Renshaw laid his hand on his arm.

'Come along, my lad,' he said gently. 'Honest men have everything to gain and nothing to lose by having their prints taken.'

Albert Mifflin shook off the grasp furiously.

'This is a free country!' he shouted. 'I protest against this — '

'Quite so,' shrugged Digby. 'But be good enough to finish your protest in the next room.'

He jerked his head towards the door and the enraged clerk was gently but firmly shepherded into the adjoining room. Then followed a half-hour of orderly but intense activity. Each man was an expert at his own particular job, and knew from the experience of many previous cases exactly what was required of him. As each completed his work and took his departure, the room gradually emptied. The first to go was the official

photographer. Before a single article had been displaced, he exposed several plates from different angles of the room and made one or two grisly 'close-ups' of the body. Then came the turn of the fingerprint expert. Using a tiny bellows and tubes of different coloured powders, white where the surface was dark and black where it was light, he carefully dusted every place likely to have been touched by the girl who had visited the office that afternoon. The handle of the weapon came in for special attention, but in spite of every portion of its polished silver surface being sprayed with the telltale powder, no sign appeared of the prints of the fingers that must have grasped it when it performed its deadly work.

'Either that hilt has been carefully wiped after the crime, or the blow was struck by a hand that was gloved,' said Inspector Renshaw. 'There's not the faintest trace of a print on it.'

Terry's heart gave an exultant leap as he heard the police officer report the negative result of the test. But the next

moment his forebodings returned with added intensity as he remembered that the only person whom he knew to have been wearing gloves was Dorene Grey.

The proceedings became less technical after the fingerprint expert had taken his departure. Inspector Renshaw threw back the plush curtains to the fullest extent and began a close examination of the windows.

One was wide open, but a single glance sufficed to show that nothing human could have entered by it, for it looked out onto a sheer drop of forty feet or so. Moreover, the thoroughfare below, although only a side street, was a fairly busy one, and would have been thronged with passers-by at the time when the crime had been committed.

The second window looked out on the main street. It was securely fastened on the inside. But the third window, on the opposite side of the room, swung open at the inspector's touch. Outside was a light iron staircase leading down into what looked like a well of blackness.

'Fire-escapes are useful things,' Sir

Digby commented, and there was a hint of dryness in his voice. 'But they are sometimes used for purposes other than saving life! See where this leads to, Inspector.'

Renshaw stepped out of the window onto to the iron rungs, and his burly figure vanished in the darkness below. In little less than a minute he was climbing back into the room.

'The fire-escape leads down into the basement, sir,' he reported, 'and there's an open door leading to a flight of stone steps giving onto the side street. The girl must have gone that way, for I found this lying on the fourth step from the bottom.'

Terry Hilton caught his breath sharply as he saw the thing that the inspector held in his hand. It was a glove of dove-coloured leather, ornamented round the edge with a distinctive border of black and white squares. It was intended for the right hand, and on the fourth finger was a thin red smear, still moist and sticky — and that was the only detail in which it differed from the gloves that Dorene Grey had been wearing when he had vainly

tried to dissuade her from keeping her appointment with Amos Rattenbury.

The Assistant Commissioner bent over the dainty relic and examined it long and carefully. Then he straightened up and reached for the telephone with one swift movement.

'I fancy this is where we let the smart lads from Fleet Street know that there's hot copy to be had for the asking,' he said thoughtfully as he lifted the receiver. 'The Gentlemen of the Press are a bit of a nuisance at times, but they come in mighty useful when it comes to spreading a net. I'll give them a full description of Miss Grey, and ask them to spread the word that she is wanted to help the police with our enquiries!'

4

The exciting events that had been crowded into the past few hours had engrossed Terry Hilton's attention to such an extent as completely to banish from his memory his brother's proposal that they should spend the evening at a theatre. When, after the last reporter had been sent on his way rejoicing, Digby reverted to the subject, he found his suggestion met with a blunt, almost horrified, refusal.

'It seems scarcely decent to think of going to a place of amusement after what we have just witnessed,' Terry said, glancing at the settee from which the body had been removed a few minutes previously. 'I've had quite enough thrills for one night, thanks!'

'Then come and have some frills, for a change,' said the less susceptible police official. 'I used to feel a bit morbid myself when first I took up criminal

investigation, but I found that there was nothing like a bright, breezy, leg-and-music show to restore a sane and balanced perspective after a gruesome homicide case. After all, Rattenbury is not such a loss to the world that we need mourn him in sackcloth and ashes!'

Terry was in no mood to contest the truth of this piece of cynical philosophy. To do so would be to betray the fact that he was not so much concerned about the fate of the murdered man as about the present whereabouts of Dorene Grey. His one desire was to seek her out, to learn from her own lips what had really happened during that fateful interview.

In spite of the evidence of the bloodstained glove, he could not bring himself to believe that the fatal stab had been delivered by her hand. The man was practically a stranger to her. She had nothing to gain by his death.

Then the haunting thought would recur: If she were innocent, why had she disappeared? Could it be possible that she was unaware that a tragedy had taken

place? In that case she would not have left by the fire escape, but through the door in the usual way. Yet if she did not kill him — who did?

In spite of his endeavours to preserve a direct line of reasoning, Terry found his available data persistently curving into a vicious circle from which there seemed no way of escape. Either he must believe Dorene to be guilty, or he must find her and learn from her own lips the explanation of this sinister mystery.

Find her! A bitter smile curved his lips as his thoughts reached this stage. With the far-flung tentacles of the most efficient police organization in the world already barring every avenue of escape, Dorene Grey would be found soon enough! And then?

With listless indifference Terry allowed himself to be carried westward in his brother's private car.

'Where shall we go?' asked Digby

'Anywhere you please,' the younger man returned curtly. 'There is not a show in London that will hold my attention tonight.'

Sir Digby favoured him with a quizzical glance.

'Don't be too sure of that, my lad,' he said with a sly chuckle of amusement. 'Have you forgotten that your latest and greatest film (for it is always the greatest until the critics begin to pull it to pieces) is to be shown for the first time at the Pantheon tonight? Do you want me seriously to believe that you're not keen on being present at your own first night performance? Especially as it is the most ambitious role that you have ever played.'

'The character of Hamlet is the most ambitious role that any actor could possibly play,' Terry returned dryly. 'And when the curtain has fallen on his performance he has either reached the top ranks of his profession or has gone to swell the number of its failures.'

'That ought to make you all the more keen on seeing what kind of reception the public gives to your particular interpretation of the character.' Digby Hilton leaned back on the cushioned seat and blew a cloud of smoke as he went on thoughtfully: 'Clifford Baxter deserves to

make a pile of money out of his experiment — if only as a reward for his pluck. But I have grave doubts about it. Artistically he may score a success, but financially — ' Digby finished the sentence with a despondent shrug. 'It's common knowledge that Shakespeare never pays.'

The Pantheon was the newest and largest of the many super-cinemas that had recently sprung up in the West End of London. Occupying an imposing corner site, the structure was not without a certain gracious dignity. In spite of the important part which steel girders had played in its construction, the whole of its exterior had been conceived on bold classical lines and skilfully adapted to the exigencies of modern requirements without a single jarring note.

The car stopped before the wide flight of steps, which swept upwards between huge Doric pillars, and Terry chuckled as he pointed to the 'House Full' notices, which were flaunted like banners of triumph over each entrance.

'I told you it would be a bumper

house,' he exclaimed. 'I wonder how many modern playwrights will be able to fill the biggest theatre in London more than three hundred years after they are dead?'

Digby's inquiry at the box office met with a polite assurance that there was not a seat to be had in the house.

'How about standing room?' he then suggested, but the man shook his head.

'Absolutely full to the doors, sir.'

Terry Hilton drew out one of his visiting cards, hastily scribbled a few words on it, and requested a passing pageboy to take it to the manager of the theatre.

A few minutes later the two were being ushered into the manager's office. A stout, sleek-headed man in immaculate evening clothes was contentedly puffing a huge cigar as he totted up rows of figures in a memorandum book. His features broke into an expansive smile of welcome as he glanced up.

'Pleased to see you, Mr. Hilton,' he greeted the younger man, but his eyes narrowed as he regarded his companion.

'Meet my brother, Sir Digby Hilton, one of the shining lights of the C.I.D.,' Terry said with easy formality. 'Mr. Rotheimer is a very old professional acquaintance of mine.'

The manager rose to his feet and bowed. 'Most happy to make your acquaintance, Sir Digby — so long as you are not here in your official capacity,' he added with an oily laugh.

'I suppose there's no need for me to ask how you find business, Mr. Rotheimer?' Terry remarked with a smile. 'The financial temperature is always well above freezing point when the 'House Full' boards go up, eh?'

Rotheimer beamed. 'Yes, Terry, we're showing to capacity tonight, and that's a fact. I don't mind admitting now that I was nervous of that film, very nervous. But Shakespeare is always like that, even in an ordinary stage show. It's either a record run or a three-night flop.'

'Is Mr. Baxter in the house tonight?' asked Terry.

'The producer of the film? Sure; I was talking to him only a moment or two ago.'

A muffled bell purred and the electric lamps became perceptibly brighter. Rotheimer made for the door. 'I must ask you to excuse me now, gentlemen. They're dimming the lights in the auditorium. That means that the film is about to start. Would you care to see the show?'

'If it's not putting you to any trouble — ' began Digby, but the manager waved his protests aside.

'No trouble — not the slightest trouble in the world, I assure you, Sir Digby,' he said affably as he conducted them down a richly carpeted corridor. 'I was reserving two stalls for Amos Rattenbury and a lady friend, but I guess they're not likely to be used tonight. That is — ' he added, with a quick glance, 'if you're not scared to sit in a seat belonging to a murdered man.'

'Oh, I'm not nervous,' said Terry.

'That was a shocking business,' the manager went on, shaking his head. 'I hope they — or rather I should say you, Sir Digby — will catch the party who committed the murder. It gave me quite a

turn when I read the news in the late editions.'

The Assistant Commissioner gave the speaker a quick, sidelong glance.

'You speak very feelingly, sir,' he remarked. 'I presume that you knew the victim rather well?'

'You may well say that, Sir Digby,' said the manager, pausing at the curtained door leading into the front of the house. 'Amos was my brother. He changed his name for business reasons many years since — before the war in fact.'

He pulled the curtain aside, but the police official made no attempt to enter.

'I'm sorry to hear that the victim was a near relative of yours,' said Digby. 'Have you any idea if he had an enemy?'

'Not the slightest idea.' Almost abruptly the manager turned and beckoned to one of the young lady attendants. 'Show these gentlemen to the two vacant seats,' he said shortly, and the next moment he had hurried away.

'This way, sir,' said the girl.

At the first sound of her voice Terry's heart missed a beat and then began to

race madly. Straining his eyes, he tried to make out the features beneath the jaunty peaked cap. But the darkness baffled him.

Like a man in a dream he followed the disc of light that the girl directed on the sloping gangway, and, still wondering if his ears had deceived him, finally stumbled into the seat that had been allotted him.

'Programme, sir?' said the girl.

Terry felt for a coin, thrust it into the girl's hand and mechanically accepted the folded sheet.

'Your change, sir,' said the bafflingly familiar voice.

'Oh, keep the change,' said Terry, vainly trying to pierce the gloom.

Without heeding him, the girl bent and placed something in his hand. The next instant she was gone, and Terry was left clutching a smooth cylindrical object, which he instinctively knew to be the police whistle that he had given to Dorene Grey.

5

Terry stifled the exclamation that rose to his lips. It needed a determined effort of will to refrain from leaping to his feet and following the girl. But even in that first stunning shock of recognition he realized that she had not revealed herself to him without good cause. The implied confidence of her act sent his pulses racing with a new and delightful excitement. She would not trust the police — yet she trusted him! By revealing her identity she had placed herself wholly in his power. He had but to whisper a few words to the man by his side and her arrest would follow as a matter of course. But those words would never be spoken by him. She had trusted him, and he would not betray her trust.

As he sat there, rigid as a statue in the plush-covered seat, his brain was humming with a turmoil of bewildering happenings which refused to be fitted into

an orderly, understandable pattern. Out of the fantastic chaos but one clear fact emerged: Dorene Grey was in danger, and she was in that theatre at that moment.

He could not help admiring the daring ruse by which she had evaded pursuit and capture. He had pictured her as a hunted fugitive, slinking in the shadows and byways of the great city, or trying to slip away unobserved from one of the railway stations. Yet here she was, calmly selling programmes and showing to their seats the patrons of a crowded first-night show. The most experienced and accomplished crook could scarcely have thought of a more effective disguise.

He did not pause to speculate on how she had come to gain entry to the Pantheon, but it was obvious that she could not have gained the opportunity of donning her uniform without the know-ledge and connivance of a member of Rotheimer's staff —

Rotheimer! The name set a jarring chord of memory vibrating in his brain. The theatre manager had admitted that he was the murdered man's brother. Was

it merely chance that the girl under suspicion for the crime should have sought shelter in that very theatre? Was there a sinister thread connecting the two? Had the girl another, deeper motive in her masquerade than that of merely evading pursuit?

Greatly to his relief, his brother made no comment on his preoccupation. Indeed, Digby seemed absorbed in the tragedy that was being enacted on the screen. The play was nearing the end of the second act, where Hamlet, his solitary, sable-clad figure dimly illuminated by the flickering firelight from the wide hearth of the tapestry-hung Castle Hall, indulges in the famous soliloquy on the art of the play-actors who have just been dismissed after performing before him:

> '*O, what a rogue and peasant slave
>   am I!*
> *Is it not monstrous, that this player
>   here,*
> *But in a fiction, in a dream of pas-
>   sion,*

Could force his soul so to his own
 conceit,
That, from her working, all his
 visage wan'd,
Tears in his eyes, distraction in's
 aspect,
A broken voice, and his whole function suiting
With forms of his conceit? And all
 for nothing!'

Then it was that the audience was afforded a subtle hint of the genius of the man who had produced the film. Hitherto the embers on the hearth had been almost dead and cold; but as the cold, philosophical soul of the student gradually became kindled with the desire for vengeance so the flames on the hearth glowed brighter, leapt higher and became more ruthless in their devouring intensity — visible symbols of the hidden fires that were consuming the soul of the man who sat watching them as he evolved a plan to snare the guilty king.

47

' . . . I have heard
*That guilty creatures, sitting at a
    play,*
*Have by the very cunning of the
    scene*
*Been so struck to the soul, that
    presently*
*They have proclaimed their male-
    factions;*
*For murder, though it have no
    tongue, will speak —*'

A simultaneous gasp of astonishment rose from every person in the crowded theatre as, without warning, the film switched off into what seemed a scene from another drama altogether.

In place of the Castle Hall they saw a background of plain grey. In place of Hamlet they saw a figure enveloped in an old-fashioned Inverness overcoat whose cape gave it the semblance of some strange bird of prey. On the Figure's head was a wide-brimmed felt hat. A black mask covered its face from brow to chin.

Raising its right hand as if to command

attention, the pictured Figure spoke — not in the stately measured periods of blank verse, but in crisp, everyday prose:

'Look at me, people, but don't be alarmed,' the Figure said in a deep voice that was obviously assumed. 'For want of a better name, let me introduce myself as the Phantom of the Films. I've interrupted the programme to give an explanation — and a warning. I killed Amos Rattenbury! That's the explanation, though not the whole of it. If the police are curious to know why I killed that man, let them look inside the fireproof safe in the office belonging to the dead man. And now for my warning: Let no man, be he the police officer or private citizen, seek to discover who I am. Regard me as a shade as unsubstantial as the pictures that are now flickering before your eyes. You cannot grasp them, you cannot touch them. They pass and fade away, but their memory and their message remains. So let it be with me. Only the wrongdoer need fear to see me appear in actual bodily shape. To the public at large I will be no more than an

exciting thrill, a piquant mystery, an elusive Figure from the realms of romance, flitting across the stage and vanishing as I do now. In other words, ladies and gentlemen, I am your devoted, but by no means obedient servant — *The Phantom of the Films*!'

6

Up in the projecting-room of the Pantheon Theatre a very puzzled operator turned to his assistant.

'Bill,' he said, 'I don't claim to be an expert in blank verse, but that last bit didn't sound to me like Shakespeare.'

'Well, it's all in the film,' Bill answered defensively. 'And we're paid to put films over — not edit them.'

The obvious truth of this remark seemed to bring no comfort to the operator.

'I guess that something's got mixed up somewhere,' he said dubiously. 'Better send a whistle down to the manager and ask him if we are to carry on.'

Bill crossed the room and lifted the speaking tube from its metal clip, but before he could place it to his lips the door burst violently open and Rotheimer himself erupted violently into the projecting-room, followed closely by Sir Digby Hilton.

The manager was in a state of breathlessness that was not wholly due to the number of stairs that he had just mounted. His heavy features were pale, and bore an expression of fear as well as anger.

'What in the devil's name do you think you are playing at up here?' he demanded when he had recovered his breath. 'What's all this monkey business about the Phantom of the Films? What the blazes do you mean by switching into a different film right in the middle of a scene?'

'We didn't do any switching,' the operator answered sulkily. 'We ran the film off from the spool just as it stood. If there was anything wrong, it must have been due to faulty assembling of the strips.'

Rotheimer gave vent to a guttural imprecation.

'No amount of faulty assembling could explain the inclusion of a scene that has nothing whatever to do with the play!' he stormed. 'Didn't either of you have the sense to 'black-out' when you

saw what was happening?'

The operator shrugged.

'I'm not paid to be a blinking film critic. My job is to put over the stuff as I get it — it's quite enough to look after the projection and sound reproduction, without rewriting the blooming scenario as it goes along!'

Sir Digby drew the manager aside.

'I think the man is quite right, Mr. Rotheimer. That film has been tampered with deliberately, and I think you'll find that strip has been inserted. Can I have a look at that particular section of the film?'

'Not now. You'll have to wait a bit. The audience will start birding the show if they are kept waiting much longer.' Rotheimer moved towards the door. 'I'll just say a few words from the stage and apologize for the interruption of the programme.'

'It might be as well to hint that the whole thing was due to a practical joke,' suggested the Assistant Commissioner. 'Treat the matter lightly.'

'I guess I know my onions,' the manager answered shortly. 'This won't

be the first speech I've made from the stage.'

Rotheimer hurried away and Digby again turned to the operator.

'Is this the first time the film has been shown?' he asked.

The man looked round and favoured him with a truculent stare. 'What's that to do with you?' he growled. 'Who are you, anyway?'

'I'm the Assistant Commissioner of Police,' said Sir Digby, accompanying the information with a bland smile. 'But I am not here in my official capacity — that is, not yet. But I'm very anxious to find out just when and how that extra strip came to be inserted into the Hamlet film. That is why I asked if you ran the film through your machine previous to tonight's performance.'

The operator shook his head.

'No, and it's my belief that the film was tampered with before it left Clifford Baxter's studio.'

'When were the spools delivered to you?'

'Yesterday afternoon.'

'And where were they stored in the meantime?'

'In this room.'

'Is the door kept locked?'

'No, it has to be left open so that the fireman can make his rounds.'

'H'm.' Sir Digby stroked his chin thoughtfully. 'So any person employed in the theatre — the cleaners, for instance — or one of the attendants, could have entered during that time?'

'Yes — but it would take more than a cleaner or attendant to patch a section into a film. You need to understand the business to play those sort of tricks. Take my word for it, sir, that film was already faked before it reached this theatre.'

Sir Digby's face was very thoughtful as he descended the flights of stone stairs and passed through the iron door that communicated with the foyer of the theatre. He had advised Rotheimer to treat the matter as a practical joke, but in his own mind he knew well enough that it was no such thing. At any rate the matter could easily be put to the proof. The Phantom had told the police to search

Rattenbury's fireproof safe, and it would be sheer foolishness to ignore the gratuitous hint. Should he institute a search now, or should he wait until the morning? As he stood hesitating before a public telephone callbox, a hand fell on his shoulder. He turned to meet the smiling eyes of Terry.

'About to call off your bloodhounds, Digby?' cried the actor, with a boyish laugh.

'Eh?' The elder man was clearly startled as he jerked out the word. 'What on earth are you talking about?'

'Surely you can see that there is no point in your arresting Miss Grey now that the Phantom fellow has confessed that he committed the murder?'

'Sorry to disappoint you, young fellow, but the order for that girl's apprehension still stands. If she did not murder Rattenbury herself, she knows who did. If not, then why is she keeping out of the way? Why hasn't she come forward to clear herself of suspicion? I have a very shrewd idea that she was in that office when the fatal blow was struck.'

Terry uttered an incredulous laugh.

'And where does Albert Mifflin come in? Is *he* the mysterious Phantom of the Films?'

'I'm going to have Mifflin up at the Yard tomorrow and he's going on the grill,' said the Commissioner grimly. 'This Phantom stuff has put a new aspect on the case, and I have a feeling that we have only seen the surface of it as yet. If Mifflin is keeping anything back from us, I bet he'll be glad to cough up all he knows before I've finished with him. It's wonderful how a reluctant witness's memory improves when he finds himself in danger of standing in the dock faced with a capital charge.'

A whistle of surprise escaped Terry's lips.

'I think you're barking up the wrong tree there, dear brother,' he said, shaking his head. 'I don't credit Mifflin with possessing sufficient pluck to kill a rabbit. I simply can't picture a man like him sticking a dagger into a fellow nearly twice his size — and in the presence of a third party, if your theory is correct. And

57

don't lose sight of the fact that the position of the wound denotes that the murder was facing his victim when the blow was delivered. Mifflin, if I am any judge of character, would have effected his purpose by a treacherous stab in the back.'

'You're getting a bit too theoretical for me, my boy,' laughed Digby. 'I prefer to base my conclusions on solid facts.'

Terry Hilton grinned.

'The self-styled Phantom of the Films is not very solid, is he?' he reminded his brother. 'He merely consists of a series of figures imprinted on a strip of celluloid, and his voice is nothing more than a line of indentations running by its side. Just a shadow of a shadow — an echo of an echo. You'll be mighty clever if you can snap a pair of handcuffs on a thing like that!'

Sir Digby shrugged with the air of one who concedes an important point. 'But he doesn't become any the less a real person because he has chosen to rig himself like a modern Guy Fawkes. That conspirator's cloak, slouch hat and mask

look suspiciously like the trappings of a maniac. He could have effected his purpose just as well by an anonymous letter to the police or a communication to the Press or media.'

Terry shook his head.

'Oh, no. In neither case would his message have reached the general public. The various editors would simply consign his screed to the wastepaper basket as the vapourings of a lunatic, and you would probably do the same. Admittedly the Phantom Stunt was sensational and crudely melodramatic, but frankly, if I myself wished to make a communication to the public without laying myself open to arrest, I scarcely think I could have hit on a better plan.'

The other man nodded in a half-hearted manner and glanced impatiently at his watch.

'Maybe you're right, Terry,' he returned with a touch of impatience. 'But I have a busy night in front of me. I was about to phone the Yard and order another search of Rattenbury's office.'

'To see if there's anything inside the

safe?' exclaimed Terry; then, as the other man nodded, he went on: 'Would I be in the way if I made one of the search party?'

'Not so long as you remember that good little boys are seen and not heard,' laughed his brother. 'Come along. You may find the experience very useful if you ever have to impersonate the character of a real detective on the stage. I'll put that call through to Inspector Renshaw and join you in a few minutes.'

'Great Scott!' exclaimed the other. 'Has that poor blighter got to turn out again? Don't you fellows ever sleep?'

A bleak smile passed across Sir Digby's features.

'Some people are of the opinion that we do nothing else,' he retorted grimly as he disappeared into the callbox.

He emerged a few moments later and looked at Terry.

'No use getting there before the others,' he said easily. 'We'll be in plenty of time if we walk.'

The night was hot and breathless, with heavy storm clouds sweeping out the

stars. As they crossed Piccadilly Circus a low mutter of distant thunder made itself heard above the noise of the traffic, and Terry, glancing down the hill towards the Duke of York's Steps, saw the towers of Westminster outlined against a fitful flicker of lightning low down in the southern sky.

Although it was long past the usual hours of business, most of the shop windows were illuminated. Scintillating sky-signs of many-coloured electric lamps proclaimed unceasingly the merits of Somebody's Whisky, the exquisite flavour of Somebody's Cigarettes, the necessity of using a Certain Brand of Gin to put the kick into the cocktail, and — possibly to correct the after-effects of a too liberal patronage of the foregoing commodities — the fiery writing on the wall flashed forth an endless repetition of the fact that Blank's Liver Salts would put you right and keep you right.

'The Lights of London — up-to-date,' Digby remarked with an upward jerk of his head. 'In the past we have had a Stone Age, a Bronze Age and an Iron Age, but

this is decidedly the Age of Advertising. And now even the crooks have been bitten by the craze for publicity.'

'It pays to advertise,' Terry quoted, smiling.

'Not in every case,' the other replied sharply. 'This so-called Phantom of the Films may pay very dearly for his rashness. In spite of his precautions, he has presented us with one or two valuable clues. We know, for instance, that he must be a man who has access to a film studio, and that he possesses some dramatic ability. Although his figure was disguised by the loose-caped overcoat, we may be able to estimate his height to within an inch or so. Most important of all, we know that he must have an accomplice; for it is obvious that he could not take a photograph of himself.'

'Sorry to dash your hopes, old chap,' said Terry, 'but your so-called clues amount to just nothing at all. You don't need an elaborately fitted studio to take a picture of a single figure and it's the hardest task in the world to judge a person's real height from a photograph,

especially when there are no accessories or articles of furniture in the picture on which a scale of comparative measurements could be based. With a background of plain grey, you can make an average man appear a giant by placing the camera low down, or reduce his height by elevating it. It's one of the tricks of the trade. Moreover, the great majority of the recording cameras used nowadays are motor-driven. It would be quite a simple matter for one man to adjust the focussing and lighting, set the machinery in motion, and then get in front of the camera and do his stuff without the aid of another person. So I shouldn't build too much on the theory of an accomplice.'

Sir Digby drew meditatively at his cigar. His face bore the expression of a man thoroughly puzzled.

'The amazing and incredible thing is that this unknown slayer should have gone to such pains to proclaim his guilt,' he said after a long pause. 'That film must have been faked long before the murder was committed, so we can dismiss the theory that the Phantom was merely

desirous of clearing Miss Grey. Apparently this man made up his mind to kill Rattenbury several days ago. Then, before the crime is committed, he makes a film in which he declares, 'I have killed Amos Rattenbury', and very neatly inserts the strip in the film of *Hamlet*, which, presumably, he knows will be shown for the first time tonight. Between five o'clock and half-past, on the same afternoon, he enters the office of his prospective victim and effects his purpose. At eight o'clock the film is shown and in due course the revelation, or confession, or whatever you like to call it, is thrown on the screen of the Pantheon Theatre. Now, tell me honestly, doesn't such a sequence of happenings strike you as being very strange?'

'Very strange,' agreed Terry, but he added quickly, 'though apparently true. The Phantom seems to have been very sure of the murder being committed without a hitch to have given notice of it beforehand, so to speak. He must have laid his plans remarkably well.'

Sir Digby laughed sardonically.

'You put the matter much too mildly, my dear Terry. Think of the small margin of time that he allowed himself — the murder at 5.30, the film at 8 o'clock. Think of the many things that might have occurred to prevent him carrying out his plan. Even as it was, Rattenbury was engaged in interviewing a client at the time the crime was committed. What would have happened if there had chanced to be more than one person with him at that time? Or was Miss Grey's prearranged presence there part and parcel of the plan?'

'Nonsense,' exclaimed Terry. 'A man as determined and as clever as the Phantom has shown himself to be, could very well dispense with such assistance as a young girl could give him.'

'I'm not so sure of that.' Digby fingered his chin thoughtfully. 'Her part in the scheme might have been to ensure that the victim was not engaged with another caller at the time the tragedy was timed to take place. That's an important part, you know.

'Why does she not come forward if

65

she's innocent?' Digby resumed. 'Why does she remain in hiding? She must have witnessed the crime. She must have seen the fatal blow struck. She must have been face to face with the Phantom in that room — '

'But how could she foresee that he was about to confess to the crime? How could she possibly guess that the film was about to be shown to the world at the Pantheon Theatre? Perhaps she has disappeared because she feared being accused. Come, tell me frankly now: if she had given herself up and told you a story of the murder having been committed by a fantastic cloaked and masked Phantom of the Films, would you have believed her? Of course you wouldn't! Would a judge and jury believe such an improbable yarn? Can't you imagine the tone of voice in which the counsel for the prosecution would ask: 'Do you seriously ask the gentlemen of the jury to credit this highly mysterious and melodramatic assassin with a real existence?' Upon my word, all things considered, I think Miss Grey is very

sensible in keeping out of the way of the police!'

Sir Digby favoured his brother with a long quizzical stare.

'Sometimes you are rather obvious, Terry,' he said slowly.

Then he added pointedly, 'Is the girl really as good-looking as all that?'

Before the young actor could think of a retort suitably cutting they arrived at their destination. As they glanced up at the silent and deserted block of offices, Digby uttered an exclamation.

'Hullo! The inspector has beaten us to it, after all. Look there!'

Following the direction of his brother's pointing finger, Terry saw a disc of white pass across the window of Rattenbury's office. Nothing but the beam of an electric torch could produce such an effect.

'Quick work,' he commented. 'Your traditional bloodhounds of the law must have been crossed with racing whippets to — '

He broke off abruptly as he felt his arm seized by a grip that made him wince.

'Quiet!' Digby's voice was tense with

suppressed excitement as he whispered the word. Drawing his brother into the shadow of the recessed doorway he went on rapidly: 'There's some queer business going on here. Renshaw's car would keep to the main streets — it's the nearest route between here and the Yard — and if he had passed us we should have spotted the car. Whoever may be up in that office, it's certainly not the police! It looks as if some other interested party has heard the Phantom's message, and is making a determined bid for the secret hidden in the safe.' He stood for a moment in thought, then: 'We'll need more men than Renshaw will bring with him. The place will have to be surrounded. I'll wait here till Renshaw — '

He finished with a gasp of dismay as the sound of a car starting into motion came from the narrow street running by the side of the block.

'Fool that I am! — I forgot the fire ladder!'

Together the two dashed round the corner, but only to see the tail-light of a powerful-looking dark green roadster

rapidly receding down the dimly lighted street.

Both men realized that any attempt at pursuit would be hopeless. In a few seconds the car had disappeared in the direction of Kingsway.

'I've got its make and number,' Sir Digby said, hastily jotting down some figures in his notebook. He tore out the sheet and handed it to his brother. 'Nip along to the nearest telephone and ring up the Flying Squad Department at the Yard. Order them, in my name, to broadcast a general hold-up order for that car. Unless the plate was a fake, and could be easily changed, the midnight visitor to the dead man's office ought to be rounded up within an hour.'

Chief-Inspector Renshaw arrived soon afterwards. He was accompanied by two officers in plain clothes, one of whom carried a leather suitcase, which gave forth the chink of metal as he lifted it from the car. Sir Digby uttered a short laugh as he heard the sound.

'I see you've brought some safe-breaking tools,' he said to Renshaw. 'But I

don't suppose they'll be needed now!' In a few words he described the light he had seen inside the building and the flight of the man in the dark green car. 'I'm prepared to bet quite a lot of money that we'll find that safe already opened.'

The Inspector had retained the keys, and a few seconds sufficed for the party to effect an entrance. Accompanied by Terry, who had hastened back after performing his errand, they made their way to the inner office. The moment he caught sight of the large green-painted safe Digby knew that his fears were realized. The door stood slightly ajar, its lock a tangled mass of torn metal.

'Hullo!' He paused suddenly before pulling the door wide open, and examined the jagged edges of the metal. 'This doesn't look very much like the work of an expert.'

Inspector Renshaw rubbed his chin.

'Well, it's hard to say, sir. These fireproof safes are not built to withstand tools. They are practically nothing but double shells of thin metal, one inside the other, the space between being filled with

a fire-resisting composition. An amateur could have done this job almost as well as a professional crook — it would be almost as easy as ripping open a sardine tin,' he concluded with a snort of contempt as he drew his flashlight and set its probing beam into the interior.

'Empty, of course?' the Commissioner asked.

'There's something white — a document — '

It was the work of an instant to fling wide the shattered door. With eager fingers Sir Digby straightened out the folds of thick, parchment-like paper and read the first paragraph of the closely-typed words.

It was the theatrical contract drawn up between Amos Rattenbury and Miss Dorene Grey, and signed by her, whereby she engaged to play a part in a forthcoming film comedy 'to the best of her skill and ability.'

But it was not the sight of the girl's name, or that of the dead man's, that made Sir Digby's eyes suddenly contract and harden to points of steel. Scrawled

across the document in red pencil were the grimly significant words:

Cancelled — by the Phantom of the Films!

7

For a full minute the Assistant Commissioner remained in silent, frowning thought, with his strange find still held in his hand. Then he slowly shook his head.

'Very startling and melodramatic,' he observed with a faint smile. 'But I don't think this clue will lead us very far — at least, not in the direction we wish to go.'

'You mean that you suspect this to be a fake designed to lead us away from the real criminal?' Renshaw asked incredulously.

Sir Digby's face was grim as he gave a slight shrug.

'Although I don't profess to be one of those marvellous detectives of fiction who make it a rule to disregard the obvious in the way of clues, I must confess I have a profound distrust of the obvious when it points to the impossible. It is an elementary truism that a single straw will show the trend of the current of a large

river, and so long as the straw is drifting with the current I am quite content to take it at its face value. But when I see a straw moving in the *reverse* direction to the flow of water, I immediately begin to suspect that some interested party must be manipulating beneath the surface. Leaving allegory and coming down to plain facts, what do we find? First we have the discovery of a lady's glove near the scene of the crime, which seems to point to a member of the fair sex having forcibly inserted about six inches of cold steel into a man's body. And now we have a safe ripped open — apparently with as much ease as one would cut a slice of bread — for the purpose of cancelling a contract that the owner of the glove had signed a few hours since. Do you for an instant imagine that a girl could have mauled that safe about in such a manner?'

Renshaw turned again to the safe, gave a tentative thrust to one of the fragments of bent iron, then shook his head.

'She'll need to be a hefty lass to have done that job,' he agreed; then his face

brightened. 'Perhaps she had a pal?'

Digby shook his head.

'There was only one person in the car,' he said with quiet decision. 'Depend upon it, these obviously feminine clues are so many red herrings drawn across the trail for our special benefit.' Into his calm voice there crept a note of rasping menace as he added: 'But our highly ingenious bluffer may find that it is a dangerous pastime handling red herrings when the pack of hounds is in full cry!'

Terry remained discreetly in the background while the detectives subjected the room to a close and methodical examination. But the only important fact that their search brought to light was that the intruder had gained entry by climbing the fire escape and forcing back the catch of the window.

'A woman could have managed *that* part of the business — or a child, for that matter,' said Inspector Renshaw as he examined the scratches on the frame of the window by the light of his flashlight. 'A single push with the blade of a knife inserted between the top and bottom

frames would be sufficient to open an old-fashioned catch like this. Almost as easy as walking through an open door. I remember once, when I was stationed at Bethnal Green — '

The sudden shrilling of the telephone cut off the remainder of the inspector's anecdote like the stroke of a knife. Sir Digby crossed the room, unhooked the receiver and placed it to his ear.

'Is that Amos Rattenbury's office?' asked a man's voice

'Yes,' said Digby.

There was a slight pause, then:

'Who is speaking?' asked the voice.

'Who is speaking your end?' demanded Digby in his turn.

'I am Sergeant Powell, of the Mobile Section, C.I.D. I've got the man in the dark green car, sir. Picked him up as he was about to cross Westminster Bridge. The general appearance of the car and the number of its registration plate tallies with the description that was broadcast from Headquarters, so I pulled him up and questioned the driver. He admitted that he had come straight from that street

leading into Kingsway, so I brought him along to the Yard.'

'Is his license in order?'

'Seems all right, sir. At any rate, the name on it corresponds with the name he gave. He wants to know what he's charged with.'

'Don't tell him,' said the Commissioner quickly. 'Just hold him till I come. I'll be along directly.'

The receiver clicked home and Digby turned to the inspector. His eyes were shining and there was a flush of excitement on his cheeks as he recounted the gist of the conversation. Such a prompt detention of the wanted man exceeded his most sanguine expectations, and he registered a mental note that Sergeant Powell's smartness should not pass without official recognition.

'They have pulled in the man whom we saw leave these premises — or perhaps it would be more correct to say after he had left the premises,' he explained. 'I'm going to Headquarters to see what he has to say for himself, but there's no need for you to leave here yet. I want this room

turned upside down and inside out. Take up the carpet, turn the pictures — '

'They want turning,' muttered the inspector with a glance of disapproval at a particularly festive work of art hanging over the fireplace.

'Sound the floors, tap the walls, and probe the upholstery of the furniture. I want this office combed through in such a fashion that there will be no question of another important piece of evidence having been overlooked. And don't forget to put a footrule over the inside and outside of this desk. There are such things as secret drawers in real life, as well as in sensational novels, you know.'

'Very good, Chief.' The inspector removed his hat and coat with a businesslike air. 'I'll make this place look like 'Home, Sweet Home' when the annual spring cleaning is let loose!'

Leaving the policemen to their task, Digby and his brother took their departure. The eyes of the older man were clouded with thought as he parted from his brother at the corner of the street. He was speculating on the identity of the

mysterious safebreaker in the dark green car — the man who had acted so promptly and so effectively after the public announcement had been made by the self-styled Phantom of the Films.

8

Arrived at the Yard, Sir Digby immediately sent for Sergeant Powell, of the Mobile Section. The sergeant was a youngish-looking man with a quiet yet alert manner. In a few words he repeated the story of the detention of the suspected man.

'Did he make any fuss when you asked him to come with you?' Digby asked at the conclusion.

'Seemed surprised, sir. That was all.'

'Made no secret of the fact that he had just come from the street off Kingsway?'

'Oh, no, sir.'

'Very good. Send him in.'

Presently there was ushered into the room a stout, round-faced man of fifty or so, with shell-rimmed spectacles and a bald head. His manner betrayed not the least sign of nervousness and his expression was that of a man who enjoys a

novel, and rather interesting, experience.

'Have I the honour of addressing one of the Famous Five?' he said in a tone of polite inquiry.

'I am one of the Assistant Commissioners of Police,' Digby answered, a trifle stiffly. 'And I should like to ask you a few questions.'

'Really?' The little man bobbed his head as though the desire for information implied a compliment. 'I am delighted to be of service to our guardians of law and order. Delighted, sir, delighted. Any advice that I can possibly give is unreservedly at your disposal — '

'It's information rather than advice that we're after,' said Digby shortly. 'Information about yourself.'

'About me?' The little man's smile grew even more genial. 'Now that's awfully good of you to take such an interest in such an unimportant, it might almost be said, such an obscure person as myself. But I sincerely trust that you are not mistaking me for somebody more important?'

'I trust so, too,' returned Digby dryly.

'First of all I should like to know your name.'

'Cyril Boyd-Pennington. You spell it with a hyphen.'

'And your address?'

'Fishlake Lodge, Blackheath.'

'Lived there long?' the police officer asked casually.

'Twenty years,' nodded Mr. Boyd-Pennington, 'since before the war. My own house. Built it myself — '

'Quite so, quite so,' interposed Digby, and at the same time he favoured the man with a long, appraising look. If this man was acting a part then he was doing it exceedingly well. 'Do you follow the news, Mr. Boyd-Pennington?' he asked suddenly.

'Most certainly.'

'Then probably you are aware that a murder was committed at number 177b New Cambridge Street this afternoon?'

Boyd-Pennington shook his head with an expression of horror.

'Yes, a shocking affair. It is appalling to think that one of our fellow creatures could be brutally done to death in the

heart of a crowded and well-policed city like this. I sincerely hope and pray that the guilty party will be brought to justice.'

Sir Digby Hilton fixed his eyes on the speaker's face.

'It may be a help towards that happy consummation if you were to explain what you were doing in the office of the murdered man some two hours since.'

'I?' An expression of bland amazement spread over Boyd-Pennington's fleshy features as he squeaked out the word. 'I in the office of the murdered man? Is this some obscure form of jest, sir? What on earth should I be doing in such a place at such an hour?'

'That is what I'm trying to find out,' said Digby grimly. 'You admitted to the officer who apprehended you that you had come straight from Little Cambridge Street, which runs by the side of the block in which Rattenbury's office is situated.'

'Certainly I did,' was the unruffled answer. 'And I spoke the truth.'

'What was your business there?'

'Oh — er — just business.'

Sir Digby frowned. 'I'm afraid I must

press for a more detailed answer than that.'

For the first time an expression of impatience passed over the placid features of the man under interrogation.

'When I said business, sir, I meant the business, profession or avocation by which I earn my living,' he explained with some dignity. 'I discovered that I had left an important plan in my office in Little Cambridge Street. I returned, got it, and came away. Is there anything criminal in that, pray?'

'Did you say, your office in Little Cambridge Street?' Digby asked in a slightly less assured tone.

'Such were my words, sir.' The little man fumbled in the breast pocket of his overcoat and drew out a bulky assortment of papers. From his vest pocket he produced a card-case and offered one of the slips of engraved pasteboard to the police officer. 'Here is my card, with my name and address of my place of business. The letters after my name stand for 'Associate of the Institute of British Architects, and Member of the Society of

Structural Engineers'. My office, number 1 Little Cambridge Street, happens to be situated directly opposite the side elevation of the premises occupied by Mr. Amos Rattenbury. That is the only connection — if, indeed, one can call it such — that I have ever had either with the murdered man or his office.'

It was only necessary for Sir Digby to glance through the sheaf of documents that the other offered to be convinced that the man was speaking the truth. There were contract notes, builders' estimates, rough plans and other obviously genuine evidences of the man's profession. Most conclusive of all were the completed plans of a large, double-fronted shop, which had been the reason for Boyd-Pennington's belated return.

There was nothing else to be done except to explain that the man's detention was due to an unfortunate mistake, and this Sir Digby did in a few well-chosen words. But even as his lips were framing the tactful apology, other singularly disquieting thoughts were hammering at his brain.

9

When Terry Hilton parted with his brother he had no intention of making his way homewards. Hailing a passing taxi, he ordered the man to drive him back to the Pantheon Theatre. The performance was over when he arrived, and the audience had already quitted the building. But he knew that the theatre staff have certain duties to perform before they leave, and he hoped to intercept Dorene and if possible learn from her own lips some explanation of the web of mystery in which she seemed enmeshed.

He took his stand at a spot where he could watch the stage door without being observed. After a few minutes' wait he saw Clifford Baxter emerge and take his departure in his magnificent limousine — evidently he had stopped behind to have a few words with the manager.

Then, by ones and twos, the theatre staff began to stream out and hurry away.

Last of all came the well-remembered figure of Dorene Grey.

Terry was on the point of stepping eagerly forward when he paused and drew sharply back into the shadow of the shop doorway.

He had caught sight of two men who were evidently following the girl. Dorene Grey was being trailed!

The young actor's jaw set tight as he considered this new and unforeseen complication. Were the two shadowers police detectives? That was the most natural explanation, but it was far from satisfying Terry. There was something furtive and sinister about their movements that did not quite fit the theory that they were engaged in a lawful enterprise.

Quickly his decision was taken. He, too, could play the shadowing game. He would track the trackers, and see whither the chase led. Terry glided from his hiding place and with swift, noiseless steps fell into the rear of the strange procession.

The girl ahead turned into a quiet, deserted side street, and the two men

immediately quickened their steps. They seemed to have thrown off all pretence of concealment as they hurried towards the girl, who, after one startled glance over her shoulder, broke into a run. Terry saw that she seemed to be making for a large car parked further up the street. He could just discern the figure of a man at the wheel. Evidently the car was waiting for her.

As he too realized this, a cry of rage burst from the foremost man. Terry's eye caught a dull glitter of metal in his outflung hand.

'Drop that!' roared Terry, and sprang forward with the alacrity of a cat.

The man with the revolver half-turned at the unexpected shout, thus conveniently exposing his jaw to the smashing right hook which Terry had ready for him. The fellow sank to the ground in a sprawling, cursing heap and the next moment the revolver was in Terry's possession.

The second man paused irresolutely as the young actor covered him with his newly-won weapon.

'Get your hands up!' he ordered crisply.

'Don't shoot, Guv'nor,' the fellow whined. 'The lady's safe. Look at 'er!'

Still keeping the revolver trained, Terry contrived to slew his eyes round sufficiently to see a large saloon car drawing up at the kerb within a yard of where he stood.

'Get in, Mr. Hilton,' the girl's voice invited from the unlighted interior.

Terry hesitated.

'How about these two beauties?' he asked, indicating his late antagonists with a wave of his weapon.

'Let them go,' she shrugged carelessly. 'They will not dare molest me again now that they know I have an armed protector.'

Slipping the revolver into his pocket, Terry Hilton obeyed.

His mind was humming with a new and disturbing train of thought as he entered the car and took his seat by the side of Dorene Grey. Immediately the great car sprang to life, and before a word was spoken it had turned into Piccadilly and was gliding rapidly westward.

Terry waited patiently for his companion to begin the conversation; but as she remained silent he felt that he had better take the initiative.

'Who? — and why?' he said softly, as though he were communing with himself.

The girl started and stared. 'I beg your pardon?'

'I fear that I was speaking my thoughts aloud, Miss Grey. When I said 'Who?' I was speaking on the identity of the two blackguards who attacked you just now. The 'Why?' was connected with the same incident.' He looked at the glass partition dividing the girl and himself from the uniformed driver. 'And I might add that I'm wondering whose car this is, and where we are going.'

She bent towards him and levelled a pair of very steady blue eyes straight into his.

'The car belongs to a friend of mine, and we are going to see him. But would you believe me if I told you that I am as much in the dark as you are as to the answers to those two first questions?' she said slowly. 'If I was to hazard a guess, I'd

say they were just opportunist thieves, who saw me leave the theatre alone, and followed me. Fortunately for me, you showed up at just the right time.'

He met her gaze with one so eager and ardent that her own eyes faltered and dropped beneath his.

'My dear young lady, the very fact of my presence here should prove to you that I'm quite willing to believe whatever you like to tell me.'

'Indeed?' Her lips were curved in a smile that seemed faintly satirical. 'You may possibly find your faith stretched to the breaking point when you have heard all I have to say.'

Terry Hilton gave a boyish laugh. 'There is only one thing you can tell me that I will refuse to believe.'

'And that is — ?'

'That you killed Amos Rattenbury.'

The lines of her beautiful face grew tense and she shivered as though at a sudden ice-cold wind.

'That is the question I have been dreading!' She broke off, with a strangled sob, and covered her face with her hands.

It was some minutes before she could continue. 'But you are right, Mr. Hilton,' she resumed in a calmer voice. 'I did not kill Amos Rattenbury.'

'But you know who did?'

She shook her head quickly, almost fiercely.

'I know as much — or as little — as the rest of the world. My knowledge begins and ends with the message that was spoken in the film at the Pantheon Theatre that night, when the self-styled Phantom of the Films confessed to having committed the murder.' She paused and smiled bitterly. 'I warned you that I should put your faith in me to a severe test. I can scarcely blame you if you refuse to believe me but I swear, by everything I hold sacred, that Amos Rattenbury was unharmed when I left his office.'

'By way of the fire-ladder?'

Her eyes widened slightly. 'How did you know that?'

'Your glove was found on the basement steps.'

'My glove!' The words were little more

than a breathless gasp as she sat back in the cushioned seat. 'Was that where I dropped my glove? I missed it later, and I wondered.'

'It was stained with blood,' Terry went on steadily.

His gaze was like a piercing sword, but she did not quail before it. She smiled instead — smiled with the air of one who senses the explanation of something puzzling and obscure.

'What a priceless clue!' she said in a tone of amused contempt. 'The glove of the murderess, stained with blood — real red blood — the blood of her victim! And dropped while she was flying from the scene of her crime. I wonder that they did not illuminate Scotland Yard that night in honour of their find! Who did find it, by the way? Surely not you?'

Terry's face was sombre as he shook his head.

'Chief-Inspector Renshaw, of the C.I.D., came upon it when he searched the basement. You admit that it belongs to you?'

'Why, of course.' There was a baffling smile on her lips as she took up her handbag, fumbled for a moment among its contents, and produced a white leather glove, its gauntlet edge bearing the now familiar black-and-white pattern.

Terry's eyes narrowed as he recognized it as the fellow to the one in possession of the police. A sudden feeling of helpless depression descended on him. Was the girl determined to pile up evidence against herself? Was she so sure that the confession of the Phantom of the Films would be taken at its face value that she could afford to take such risks? Was she deliberately trying to shake his faith in her?

By some subtle instinct she seemed to guess the thoughts that were seething in his brain.

'Faith still standing strong?' she queried, the mocking light dancing in her eyes. 'Or are you ready to confess that it is getting the least bit tottery? Maybe another little piece of evidence will cause it to overbalance and come crashing to the ground?'

She picked up the glove and slowly drew it on her left hand, holding it up for his inspection.

'The look in your eyes tells me that it is needless for me to ask if you recognize this glove,' she went on in a hard, passionless voice. 'I dare say you are quite prepared to go into the witness-box and swear that it is identical with the one found near the scene of the crime?'

Terry Hilton shrugged and looked away.

'What need for me to swear anything, since you admit that the other glove belonged to you?'

She shook her head as if determined that he should not evade her question. 'But is it identical?' she insisted.

'Yes,' he answered bluntly.

'Wrong!' she returned with a little laugh of triumph. 'The other glove was stained with blood — this one is quite clean. But that is a detail that is quickly remedied. See — '

She made a quick movement with her right hand, and to Terry's horror and amazement a broad streak of brilliant

crimson appeared as if by magic on the white leather.

Unheeding the startled exclamation that broke from his lips, Dorene deftly stripped the glove from her hand and tossed it across to him.

'Take that to Scotland Yard, Mr. Hilton,' she said with a laugh. 'Let them compare it with their other precious clue. Let them take both to their wonderful laboratories, examine them under the microscope, analyze them, scrutinize them — and after they are finished let them compare the result of their labours with — this!'

'A lipstick!' he cried.

There was mischievous triumph in the eyes she turned on his.

'And that is the very tame and disappointing climax of the thrilling trail of the sinister, blood-stained clue!' she said in tones of mock tragedy. 'I thought I might have to undergo a film test of some kind when I answered the advertisement, so I bought some make-up on my way from the station. Unfortunately I grasped the tube too tightly while endeavouring to

unscrew the cap, and the wretched stuff oozed out all over my fingers. I tried to rub it off with my handkerchief, but it seemed to stick like glue — '

'No wonder!' Terry interposed, glancing at the label of the tube. 'It says here that the stuff is 'Guaranteed Kissproof'.'

Dorene Grey's colour heightened suddenly and she looked away.

'The late Mr. Rattenbury seemed inclined to put that guarantee to a practical test,' she said with a shudder. 'That's why I thought it best to make my exit by the fire-escape without waiting to indulge in formal adieux.'

'He did not attempt to follow you?' Terry asked quickly.

'I really did not wait to see. I was too eager to get out of that horrible room. You were quite right when you described that man as a beast.'

'Did he come as far as the window?'

The girl remained in thought for a few seconds, then nodded her head.

'Yes. I remember hearing him calling to me as I descended the fire-escape. He was trying to induce me to come back, I

think. I heard him say something which sounded like, 'Now's your chance — you'll make a certain hit', or words something like that. I glanced up and saw him leaning out of the open window, but by the time I had reached the foot of the ladder he had disappeared.'

'Are you sure that it was actually Rattenbury who said those words about making a certain hit?'

Dorene's eyes widened in surprise.

'Why, who else could it have been?' she cried.

Terry did not answer her for a moment. Something in her recital of her escape had started a novel train of thought in his mind. It was only natural that the girl, assuming the words to have been spoken by Rattenbury, had jumped to the conclusion that they referred to the contract that she had just signed. Certainly, 'You'll make a certain hit' was the usual phrase in which one member of the theatrical profession might express his confidence in the coming success of another. But, regarded in the light of what must have happened within a few seconds

of her quitting the room, the words might have had a more literal, more sinister meaning. What if the 'chance' was the chance of taking the victim unawares, and the 'certain hit' the swift dagger-stroke which ended his life?

Resolutely thrusting his suspicions into the background for the time being, he returned an evasive answer and at once steered the conversation into a different channel by remarking:

'But you haven't explained how you came to be selling programmes in the Pantheon Theatre that night.'

The girl smiled faintly. 'It's simply explained. When I arrived in London yesterday, I had the evening to kill before my interview with Mr. Rattenbury today — so I decided to visit this cinema. I arrived between performances, and passed the time waiting by studying the film posters in the foyer. Mr. Rotheimer noticed me, and introduced himself as the manager. We got to chatting, and he asked me what I was doing in London. When I told him of my intention of seeing Mr. Rattenbury the next day, he seemed very

interested — even concerned. He said that if my interview did not work out, I should come back to the cinema and ask to see him. He had contacts in the film business, and said he might be able to help me find work.'

'More than likely he could,' Terry said thoughtfully. 'So, after your brush with Rattenbury, that's just what you did?'

The girl shook her head. 'Not at first. Fleeing Rattenbury's unwanted attentions, I found myself in the street after descending the fire-ladder, and my one thought was to get back to my flat as quickly as possible. I do not think there was a more disillusioned girl in the whole of London than I at that moment. The thought of Rattenbury filled me with disgust. Were all film producers of his type? I wondered; or was he just one of the black sheep that are to be found in every fold? At any rate I had had enough of the cinema business for one day. The very atmosphere of that horrible room made me feel unclean. I was so upset I just didn't know *what* to do. At first I just sort of wandered around, going to various

cafés and Coffee Bars. It must have been nearly two hours later, after I had calmed down, when I suddenly remembered about Mr. Rotheimer's offer to help me. I went to the Pantheon Cinema and asked to see him, and I was shown to his office there.' The girl paused, wrinkling her brows.

'When I went into his office I found him reading an evening paper. He seemed very agitated. Well, I was about to tell him what had happened to me, but he cut me short, and asked me if I'd seen the story in the evening paper. When I said I hadn't he thrust the paper at me. I was horrified to read there that Mr. Rattenbury had been found stabbed, and that the police were looking for me, as the last person known to have seen him — '

'My brother had great hopes that you had encountered the Phantom face to face in Rattenbury's office,' Terry cut in. 'Or that you had seen him on the fire-escape, and I rather fancy that he was hoping you'd be able to give a more detailed description than the muffled and

disguised figure which appeared on the film.'

The girl shook her head.

'I did not encounter a single soul until I had gained the side street which runs by the side of the block of offices. There were plenty of passers-by there, of course, but I did not take notice of any one in particular. I had no reason for doing so, for at the time I had no idea that the murderer had climbed the fire-ladder leading to the room I had just quitted.'

Terry Hilton frowned as he fingered his chin thoughtfully.

'Then how on earth did the Phantom get in to do the dirty work?' he frowned. 'The police have turned that office upside down and inside out. They have stripped the walls and tested every floorboard. Two of the windows open out onto the sheer face of the building, overlooking a crowded street. The other window faces a side street, which is slightly less crowded, it is true, but if the murderer had climbed the fire-ladder leading to it he must have been seen by you. That leaves the door as the only other possible means of entering

— and Mifflin was within sight of that all the time,' he concluded with a helpless shrug. 'If the Phantom of the Films managed to enter the room, commit the crime, and have left it unseen within the space of a few seconds — well, he must be a phantom in something more than name!'

The girl made no reply, but continued to gaze with deep-brooding eyes at the dimly lighted suburban streets through which the car was gliding.

'Please go on with your story,' Terry urged. 'You're doing fine.'

'Mr. Rotheimer said that I dared not go to the police, because they clearly suspected me. He suggested that I should lie low in his cinema, undercover as an usherette, whilst he thought out what I ought to do next. My head was in a whirl, so naturally I agreed — but when I saw you, Terry, I thought that you might be able to help me, without giving me away. So I returned that police whistle you'd given me . . .

'Then, after the film was run and the Phantom's confession was made public,

Mr. Rotheimer seemed very relieved. He told me that I should no longer be afraid of the police. He asked me if I had any family or friends I would like to telephone to put their minds at rest — in case they'd heard about the police looking for me. Of course, I had no immediate family, but then I thought about my father's great friend, Professor Dangelli. I used Mr. Rotheimer's office phone to call him, and I explained what had happened. He seemed to know all about it, and he said that he wanted to see me urgently. He said he would send his chauffeur, Vincenzio, to pick me up outside the cinema in his Daimler. I was on my way to the car, when I was attacked by those two thugs. Had it not been for you helping me, I might have been in a tight corner!'

'Has it not occurred to you, Miss Grey, that you might have found yourself in an even tighter corner had not the Phantom come forward with his public admission of guilt?' Terry remarked. 'All things considered you should feel rather grateful to him than otherwise. His confession

clears you of the least suspicion of having committed the murder.'

'Are you sure it does?' Dorene shrugged wearily. 'What if the police refuse to believe that confession?'

'Why should they refuse to believe it?' he demanded warmly.

'Because a confession of a man who withholds the vital fact of his own identity is practically no confession at all in the eyes of the law. The Phantom of the Films is the shadow of a shadow; his so-called confession a mere echo of an echo. He might be anybody or nobody. A lay figure behind which anyone might hide. Given a cloak, a mask, and a talent for speaking in a peculiar tone of voice, the Phantom might be you, or I, or anybody else.'

Terry Hilton shook his head obstinately.

'But the Phantom is at least — '

He got no further, for at that moment the car stopped. Glancing through the window, Terry could discern not the slightest sign of human habitation.

'Where are you taking me?' he asked.

'I'd like to introduce you to my friend

Professor Dangelli. I'd mentioned to him on the phone how you had tried to warn me about seeing Mr. Rattenbury, and he said he'd be interested in meeting you. Although he does not advertise his successes, he is the foremost scientific criminologist of the present day. He is very rich, very clever, and very eccentric. His one passion in life is the solving of intricate crime mysteries; his one aversion is the organized police force of this country, the individual members of which he regards as so many unimaginative and ignorant blunderers. Nothing pleases him better than to succeed where they have failed.'

'But why on earth does he want to see me?' inquired the wondering Terry. 'Surely he must know that I have no official connection with the police?'

The girl's lips twitched in a laugh of tolerant amusement.

'True,' she admitted. 'It is just the very fact of your being unconnected that makes him willing to place the results of his investigation before you. He has received so many rebuffs from Scotland

Yard in the course of his previous investigations that he hates the sight of a man in uniform. Your brother, Sir Digby, has already refused the Professor's offer to help, at the same time intimating pretty bluntly that his Department does not encourage the interference of scientific cranks, and Dangelli is anxious to convince him of his mistake — through you. Don't you think that you had better see him?'

'I certainly do!' Terry answered with conviction. 'I'm quite keen on seeing this most retiring sleuth face to face. It might be interesting to find out from where he got his information. You know, Miss Grey, the very best detective in the world to unravel a murder mystery is the man who actually committed the crime!'

The girl smiled, then turned to speak to the driver of the car. 'Thank you, Vincenzio. We'll walk from here — Mr. Hilton and I are going to see the Professor now. He'll contact you again when we need a lift back to London.'

The chauffeur nodded, and touched his cap.

10

With Terry at her side, Dorene paused before a wooden gate, which, to a stranger, might have passed unnoticed amid the thick foliage of a neglected hedge. She pressed a button sunk in the woodwork, and the gate swung open without a sound. She shot a glance at Terry, who was frowning.

'I used to come to this house many a time with my father,' she explained.

A short walk through densely wooded grounds brought them to the porch of a large, square-built mansion, plain and forbidding. The car followed slowly behind them. No gleam of light came from the tightly shuttered windows; no plume of smoke, hinting at cheerful fires within, from the roof topped with ranks of chimneys which now showed dimly gaunt against the indigo sky; not even the challenging bark of a watchdog broke the deep uncanny silence which seemed to

hang like an invisible shroud over that blank-faced, brooding mausoleum of a dwelling-place.

The front door swung open as they mounted the steps. The manservant who opened it recognized Dorene, but gave Terry a puzzled glance. Quickly, Dorene gave his name and added that Dangelli had wanted to see him.

The manservant put through an internal telephone call, then:

'Professor Dangelli is at home,' the manservant informed them. 'Be pleased to follow me to the study.'

Crossing the hall, he led the way up the wide staircase, through a small lobby, which terminated in an arched door of panelled oak. Giving three taps, the servant entered.

'A lady and gentleman to see you, sir,' he announced.

'They are welcome,' wheezed a querulous, high-pitched voice from behind a high pile of books on the table. 'Come in, my dear Miss Grey and Mr. Terry Hilton.'

The man who rose to his feet at their entry was obviously a foreigner. Although

of no more than average height his figure was so thin as to make him appear extremely tall. Nor was his age less difficult to determine. The mop of pure white hair that crowned his head might have belonged to a man of eighty. But the dark restless eyes, bright as polished jet and keen as spear-points, the upright carriage and general air of robust vitality, would not have been out of place in a man of half that age. His features were thin and sallow, his eyebrows sloped upward from the bridge of his eagle nose at an angle that was almost grotesque. A short pointed beard rendered his long face longer still, and the waxed grey moustaches did not entirely conceal the straight inexorable line of his mouth. Terry, surveying him with professional interest, could not help thinking that, with his lean figure encased in a suit of rusty armour, the old professor might have stepped straight onto a stage as the immortal Don Quixote.

Nor were the man's surroundings entirely out of keeping with that legendary character, for the decorations of the

room consisted entirely of ancient arms and armour. Spaced at intervals round the walls were effigies wearing the defensive steel trappings of various historical periods. Some were encased in the complete plate armour that was worn when knightly chivalry was in full flower; some wore the chain mail of the time of the First Crusade; others displayed the lighter half-armour which followed the general introduction of firearms to the field of battle.

The walls were hung with a multitude of weapons of every description. Lances, great double-handed swords, heavy steel maces, crossbows, long-barrelled flint-lock pistols, rapiers and daggers were there in profusion, some hanging singly, some clustered so thickly that from a short distance they formed a symmetrical and not unattractive ornamental design. Terry had never seen such a collection of death-dealing implements except within the walls of a museum, and his interest was so apparent that the owner could not help noticing it.

'You are admiring my little collection,

is it not so?' he asked in a voice that betrayed the merest suspicion of a foreign accent. 'It is interesting to trace through the ages the efforts which mankind has made to perfect instruments with which to satisfy his inborn lust for blood. Stone axe, bronze dagger, iron sword, match-lock, wheel-lock, flint-lock firearms, mark the successive stages of his so-called civilization, until at the present day he has reached the crowning achievement of the bomb. Gaze on the examples of death-dealing ingenuity on those walls, and then dare to deny that Man is a progressive animal!'

For a moment Terry Hilton was at loss for an answer. The professor's utterances had been couched in terms of such biting irony that the young actor had begun to wonder if he were expected to praise or condemn the lethal weapons before him.

'As you take such an interest in instruments designed for slaying,' he said at length, 'perhaps you have evoked a theory concerning the Rattenbury murder?'

'I have,' agreed the old man. 'I consider

it to be the most baffling crime of the century.'

'The police won't thank you for telling them *that* piece of news,' Terry said soberly. 'Why not arrange an interview with my brother and place your theory before him personally?'

The old man shrugged his narrow shoulders and made an expressive grimace.

'I fear that I am not exactly *persona grata* at Police Headquarters. Your so clever English detectives do not encourage interfering amateurs who offer to teach them their business. I go to Scotland Yard. Good! The Chief Inspector in charge of the case welcomes me, asks me to be seated. He thinks he scents some 'information received' — is not that how you call it? 'What do you know about this matter?' he asks. 'Perhaps not so much as you do,' I answer, 'but I have made better use of my data.' A chilliness descends on the atmosphere. 'Oho!' thinks this excellent Inspector of Police, 'here's another crank whose bonnet is full of bees. Here is a man whose intellects

are not functioning normally.' The Inspector frowns and his manner becomes very business-like. 'Have you additional evidence to offer? Did you witness the crime?' he asks sternly. I can only tell him that I was miles away at the time. 'But I have a theory,' I add, 'a theory that I have deduced from the evidence that you already hold.' His face grows red and he makes the gritting noise with his teeth. 'We will communicate with you in due course. Good morning. This is the nearest way out.' And so the matter ends as it has ended so many times before. The good Inspector Renshaw keeps his *amour proper* — and I keep my knowledge under my hat. Everybody is satisfied — and most satisfied of all is the criminal who goes scot-free!'

'Come, come, professor. Aren't you being a little unjust?' Terry felt it incumbent of him to make some defence of his brother's department. 'I can recall hundreds of instance where the Yard has asked the opinions of experts.'

Professor Dangelli nodded quickly.

'That I am perfectly willing to concede,'

he returned with a slight shrug. 'They submit a bullet to a gunsmith. They call in a jeweller to assess the value of precious stones. They send laundry-marks to a laundry, and a suit of clothes to a tailor in order to discover the identity of the wearer. But they never dream of submitting a collection of facts respecting a crime to a scientist who has made a life study of solving mysteries. To the professional thief-taker, the amateur investigator simply does not exist — except perhaps to be derided and laughed at. And it does not amuse me to find myself the object of mirth.' The old man drew himself up and his dark eyes flashed. 'I intend to follow the example of the elusive Phantom of the Films!'

'What!' cried the startled Terry.

The professor smiled as he stroked his grey moustache with an air of prim self-satisfaction.

'Yes, my friend. I am about to commence the writing of a film scenario that, under the thinly-veiled guise of a thrilling crook-drama, will present to the British public the true solution of the

mystery of Amos Rattenbury's death. That is practically the only method by which I can make the truth known; for the newspapers would not dare to print my statement, and Scotland Yard would certainly consign it to the wastepaper basket as the vapouring of a lunatic. Did not the Phantom recognize these facts when he inserted his confession-film in the reel that was to be exhibited at the Pantheon Theatre? I will take a leaf out of his book. I will expose him by the very same medium under which he has so far hidden his identity. But, unlike him, I shall not work in secret. When the film is completed, I shall take over the lease of one of the West End theatres, and advertise the film openly. Moreover,' he went on with growing excitement, 'I shall, as far as possible, engage the same persons to play the same parts that they played in the real-life drama. Needless to say, the heroine will be played by this lady. That is why I asked her to come here tonight.'

He indicated Dorene Grey, who had been a silent but intent listener to the

conversation that had passed between the two men. 'You will of course accept the part, my dear?' he asked.

Astonished, the girl could only nod.

'Film making is a costly form of amusement,' Terry warned him but the other made a careless gesture with his hands.

'I am not exactly a poor man, Mr. Hilton, and I am sanguine enough to expect that I shall get something more than my initial expenses back when the film is released. At least I shall not have to lay out money in preliminary press notices. The police will give me all the advertisement I need.'

'In what way?'

'I shall wait until they are on the point of arresting me for the murder.' A sardonic smile played about Dangelli's lips. 'Then I will launch my bombshell!'

11

The flat in which Dorene Grey had taken her quarters was situated at the top of a tall residential block above a shop in a quiet side street near New Oxford Street. The three rooms, though small, provided ample accommodation for her needs, and their decorations and appointments were on a much better scale than she had expected from the somewhat dingy exterior of the house. Most important item of all, the rent seemed ridiculously low.

Her new quarters had proved comfortable indeed, and if her landlady was somewhat taciturn and aloof, they were qualities that Dorene appreciated rather than resented.

Mrs. Mattioli, in spite of her foreign-sounding name, was a Londoner born and bred. She was a stout, florid-faced woman with hair of that dull, lustreless yellow which chemists label 'golden'. In

striking contrast, her husband was a short, slight, sallow-skinned Italian with hair and moustache black as jet.

Dorene fancied that he must be a waiter at one of the hotels or night clubs, for he always left the house about seven o'clock at night and returned in the early hours of the morning, and on more than one occasion she had encountered him on the stairs and caught a glimpse of evening clothes beneath his overcoat.

Although she had no particular reason for reticence, she had divulged her new address to very few people. When Mrs. Mattioli knocked on her door one morning with the announcement that a gentleman had called to see her, Dorene was not so much startled as puzzled.

'Are you sure he wishes to see me?' she asked.

The landlady nodded.

'Miss Dorene Grey he asked for, as plain as he could speak.'

The girl hesitated, her eyes fixed on the neatly engraved words on the card that Mrs. Mattioli had handed to her.

The names were Cairncross and

Beeding, and beneath them was an address in Gray's Inn. They were uncommon names, and as she repeated them aloud they seemed to have a familiar ring. Swiftly her decision was made. 'Please ask the gentleman to come up,' she said.

'Good morning. Miss Grey, I presume? I am Walter Cairncross, senior partner of the firm of solicitors whose card I sent to you.'

The man who thus introduced himself was of considerable age, with snow-white hair worn rather long and a pair of short, bushy side-whiskers. His irreproachable frock coat, white waistcoat and striped grey trousers seemed to belong to an age when such a formal costume was considered indispensable while transacting business. He placed his high hat on the table, deposited a small bag of shiny black leather on the floor, drew out a pair of gold-rimmed spectacles and, settling them firmly on his high-bridged nose, subjected Dorene to a prolonged and embarrassing scrutiny.

'The resemblance is unmistakable!' he

exclaimed at last.

'I beg your pardon?' said the thoroughly mystified girl.

Instantly the old man was all apologies.

'No, my dear young lady, it is my place to beg yours for what must have sounded like an impertinent remark on my part. I was speaking my thoughts aloud — a dangerous practice for one of my profession, eh?'

'Won't you sit down?'

'Thank you Miss Grey. And I beg you to be seated also. I may want to have quite a long talk with you.'

'What about?'

The directness of the question seemed to discomfort the old gentleman. He removed the spectacles, which he had just put on, wiped them carefully with his handkerchief, replaced them and gave a little dry cough.

'The — ah — matter in hand cannot, I regret to say, be described in two words. It is connected with the — hem! — the affairs of the late Doctor Duncan Grey.'

'My father?'

The old solicitor nodded.

'But he died six months ago,' cried the bewildered girl.

'Exactly. And you, his only child, were the sole heiress to his estate.'

In spite of the sad recollections conjured up by the lawyer's words, Dorene could not help smiling.

''Heiress' seems a somewhat grandiloquent term to apply to poor little me,' she said. 'Of late years Daddy was so wrapped up in his endless experiments that I'm afraid he neglected his practice. The number of his patients fell off and when he died there was very little practice to sell. It fetched a little money when it was sold, however, and that money and the house in which we lived was the whole of my inheritance.'

There was a kindly smile on the old man's face as he slowly shook his head.

'Wherein you are mistaken, my dear Miss Grey. Your father's most valuable asset was not mentioned specifically in his will.' He clicked open his bag, groped among its contents, and selected a folded document. 'This is a copy of that will. I will read the concluding paragraph. *And I*

likewise bequeath to the beforementioned Dorene Grey any further increments to my estate that may accrue from any source whatever, the said increment to be paid to her unconditionally, for her sole use and benefit.'

As Dorene listened, a puzzled little frown crossed her forehead at intervals.

'But there were no traces of any 'further increments' when the estate was wound up,' she said with a rueful shake of her head.

'Not *then* maybe,' said the lawyer with peculiar emphasis. 'But there has been a most valuable increment since that date.'

'What do you mean?'

There was a short pause and Dorene's wondering eyes saw that the old man was regarding her very fixedly. When next he spoke there was a note of tenderness underlying his usual dry legal accents.

'I was something more to your father than an ordinary legal adviser. Years ago, before he became almost a recluse because of his passion for scientific research, I was one of his closest friends. He confided to me secrets that he

jealously guarded from members of his own family. I will not say that he gave me his fullest confidence. He could not do that — by so doing he would have betrayed matters of which he was not at liberty to speak. But I think I am well within the truth when I say that I alone — with the exception, of course, of certain highly-placed Ministers of His Majesty's Government — was the only man who knew the real import of the ceaseless experiments which he conducted in the specially-built laboratory at the bottom of the garden of his house at Highspur Heath.'

A light of understanding began to dawn in Dorene's eyes. She remembered the cold winter nights when she had lain awake and gazed from her bedroom window at the brightly illuminated window of the rambling, single-storey building in which her father was toiling at his self-appointed task. Only on one occasion had she caught a glimpse of its interior.

When little more than a child she had ventured within the forbidden doorway to

retrieve the ball with which she was playing. She remembered it as a place of dazzling light and stark black shadows; a place where innumerable glass bottles stood in rows on shelves; a place of odd corners, dark and fearsome, where queer-looking machines reflected the light from their sleekly gleaming bodies; a place of strange sounds and strange odours; and — most poignant memory of all — a place which nearly proved as deadly to the innocent intruder as the fabled forbidden chamber of Bluebeard.

Childlike, she had been fascinated by the bright green liquid, which bubbled and seethed in a retort suspended on an iron tripod above the hissing flame of the Bunsen burner. For a while she had contented herself with watching the green vapour travel through the transparent glass tubing, change colour as it passed through a wider tube, and finally distil in drops of reddish-brown liquid in a flask at the further end of the apparatus. It seemed a novel and wholly delightful toy — no wonder Daddy shut himself up for hours in order to play

with such a thing! Dorene would play with it too.

Dragging a stool across the uncarpeted floor, she had mounted it, stretched out her little hand, and grasped the section of tubing which confined the swift-moving green spirals. It was unexpectedly hot, and the sudden start of pain caused one of the rubber connections to slip from the tube. Then a great invisible hand seemed to come out of nowhere, fastening on her throat, squeezing it, tighter and tighter — until she remembered no more.

After that the door of the laboratory was fitted with a spring lock and made self-closing, and it was not until many years later that Dorene realized how near to death she had been when her father had rushed in and snatched her from that gas-filled room.

'You mean that my father had invented, or discovered, a new type of weapon for use in warfare?' she hazarded, her face very set and pale.

The face of Walter Cairncross was as grave as her own as he slowly shook his head.

'I regret that I am expressly forbidden to answer that question, Miss Grey. The only information I can give you — and even that is in confidence — is that your father invented a very potent and effective weapon of destruction shortly before he died. As a patriotic Englishman, he offered this new weapon to his own Government. That was exactly ten months ago. Your father was well aware of the fact that the War Office does not act or decide precipitously on such matters, and he was also aware of his own approaching death. So he empowered me to conduct the business part of the transaction, and in the event of his pre-decease, to see that the money was safely handed over to you. In view of the well-known fact that every will and testament can be inspected by any member of the public on application at Somerset House on payment of a small fee, he dared not make the bequest in his will in any plainer terms than those which he actually used. He had reason to think that the intelligence agents — in plainer language, the spies — of more than one

foreign nation had got wind of the fact that he was engaged in secret and highly important investigations.'

The girl nodded.

'It was common gossip in the neighbourhood. Some of the villagers used to call him 'the mad doctor',' she said in a low voice.

'Well, it's a pity we cannot confound the rustic wise-acres by giving them a glimpse of the cheque which will in due course be placed to your credit.'

'Is it for a very large amount, then?'

'Large?' Walter Cairncross chuckled. 'Well, that is a relative term, young lady. A sum which appears colossal to a private individual may seem a mere trifle to a Government which believes that a state of preparedness is the best preventive of ruinously expensive wars. Your father very wisely left the War Office to fix the price for his invention, and I will think you very greedy indeed to quarrel with their decision. I am happy to be able to inform the daughter of my old friend that she is the sole possessor of two million pounds.'

'Two million!' gasped Dorene.

At this, the woman who had been listening at her keyhole throughout the whole of the interview straightened herself up and hurried down the stairs with rapid yet noiseless tread. In the room below, Mattioli, lounging on a dingy settee with a newspaper and a cigarette, started up eagerly at her entrance.

'Well, the old boy he spill-a da beans, hey?'

The woman to whom the question was addressed allowed a few seconds to pass in silence. The constrained position that she had been forced to adopt during her recent eavesdropping had left her a little breathless.

'He told the gal that the Guv'ment had bought her father's invention for £2,000,000.'

Andrea Mottioli threw up his hands with a gesture of delighted amazement.

'*Dio mio!* Is there so much money in the world? And he did not mention the nature of this most valuable invention?'

The woman shook her head sullenly.

'Close as an oyster. Said he dared not

hint at the nature of the new weapon, even to her.'

The disappointed Mattioli gave vent to a string of sibilant curses in his native language. Presently his countenance cleared.

'But the old boy's caution — that proves that we're on something big? The Phantom, he no wrong after all.'

'Is he ever wrong?' the woman answered wearily. 'When you telephoned to tell him that the girl had arrived in London and booked in here, did he not arrange to pay three-quarters of the rent of her flat, unbeknown to her, in order to have her where he wants her *when* he wants her?'

'*Silencio!*' hissed the Italian, placing his hand over the woman's mouth and at the same time glancing apprehensively towards the closed door. Outside, the slow footsteps of Walter Cairncross could be heard passing the door as he cautiously descended the stairs. When the distant thud of the street door being closed proclaimed that the visitor had left the house, Mattioli released his hold of the woman.

Without a single glance or word of resentment she crossed to the telephone and dialed a number.

'Be careful what you say,' warned her husband. 'Sometimes people overhear — '

'I should worry!' A smile, cold and grim, played about the woman's coarse mouth. 'I'm only going to tell the Phantom that he may expect to be drawing some of the dividends on his sunk capital — and before very long, too!'

12

That afternoon Dorene Grey found herself studying the shop windows of the automobile agents and the more exclusive milliners and costumiers with a new and personal interest. A sense of pleasant bewilderment came over her as she realized that by a turn of Dame Fortune's capricious wheel the most expensive of these luxuries were within her reach. She was a rich woman now. No longer would every little item of extra expenditure have to be prefaced with a harassing arithmetical problem whose satisfactory solution depended on every single pound being made to bear the value of two.

The sight of a tattered beggar holding a few boxes of trinkets in his shaking hand brought a mute reminder that everyone was not as fortunate as she. Dorene paused before him and felt for her purse, only to give a little gasp of dismay as she realized that it was gone. Then she

remembered the man who had lurched against her when she had been looking at the posters exhibited in the window of the travel agents. His sudden stagger had led her to assume that he must be intoxicated, yet his steps had been steady enough when he had hurried away and mingled with the crowd. It was her first experience of the amazing skill of the expert pickpockets who infest certain quarters of the West End of London.

It was not the actual amount of her loss that caused Dorene's forehead to pucker into a frown of annoyance, for there had been but a few pounds in her purse. Modest though the sum was, its disappearance was likely to prove very inconvenient, for it left her, for the moment, absolutely penniless.

She had been too excited by the lawyer's announcement of her unexpected inheritance to eat much at lunch time and now, to add to her discomfiture, she was unpleasantly reminded of the fact. No sooner did it dawn upon her mind than she immediately began to feel ravenously hungry. Fortunately, there was

a way out of her predicament, though it would mean a somewhat long walk. Of course, Mr. Cairncross would be quite willing to make a small advance on her immense legacy. She would walk to his office.

The smile died on her lips as she remembered that she had placed the card bearing his address in the purse, which had been stolen. She tried to recall the neatly-engraved copperplate letters which she had read on the card: *Cairncross and* — . What was the other name? And what was the address beneath? Was it Gray's Square, or Gray's Inn or Gray's Inn Road? She shook her head in despair. The exciting news that had followed the hurried perusal of the card had quite blotted the address from her memory.

Busy with these thoughts, she walked the whole length of Piccadilly, and with some surprise found herself immediately facing the Pantheon Theatre.

TERRY HILTON in 'HAMLET'. The words caught her eyes as they flashed at intervals from the façade of the theatre in many-coloured electric lamps whose

lustre was somewhat dimmed by the still lingering daylight. Every poster echoed the same famous name. Between the two doors was a huge oil painting, an enlargement of one of the photos of the actual film, representing Terry in the well-known graveyard scene.

Dorene paused before the picture and for a long while remained gazing earnestly up at the face beneath the black-plumed hat, her surroundings forgotten in the crowd of memories which flocked unbidden to her mind.

'Not so dusty, is it?' said a bantering voice at her side and she turned to meet the laughing eyes of the original of the pictured Prince of Denmark. 'I look well done in oils — I ought to have been a sardine!'

She gave a happy, breathless little laugh, which sounded to Terry like broken music.

'For heaven's sake don't talk about sardines — or anything else that is eatable!' she begged in tones of tragedy. 'I'm starving! I've just had my pocket picked. And I feel most dreadfully

hungry,' she added desperately.

'Tough luck,' commented the young actor. 'Did you lose much?'

Dorene shook her head.

'Not much. But it was all I had with me. Of course — '

She was on the point of telling him about her unexpected legacy, but some subtle instinct of caution caused her to break off with the words unspoken. Walter Cairncross had not exactly told her to keep her good fortune a secret, but he managed to convey the impression that he expected her to do so. Fortunately, Terry did not notice her embarrassed pause.

'Have you seen the Pantheon's Tea Lounge?' he asked with a jerk of his head towards the doors of the theatre. 'Let me show it to you.'

Nothing could have exceeded the tact with which the invitation was given. But Dorene shook her head.

'Not there,' she said quickly, repressing a shudder with difficulty. 'I'm beginning to hate that theatre.'

'Yes,' said Terry as he turned away, 'I must admit that it is beginning to acquire

a somewhat sinister reputation. Let's have tea somewhere else. I know the jolliest place in London. You've heard of 'The Laughing Mask'?'

Dorene nodded. She recognized the name as that of one of the newest and smartest of those queer little clubs that seem to spring up like mushrooms in the congenial soil of the square mile immediately surrounding Piccadilly Circus. It would seem as if the promoters had chosen a suitable name for their new venture, for 'The Laughing Mask' had immediately caught on with the theatrical fraternity. Everyone in the profession was talking about it, and Dorene had a quiet natural curiosity to see for herself what this much-lauded place was really like.

'I've heard of it,' she answered with the faintest shade of hesitation, 'but I've heard that it's rather a dubious place.'

'Dubious nothing,' Terry answered contemptuously. 'The place is rather exclusive, that's all. Mattioli tries to limit his clientele to members of the theatrical profession, and the non-professional

people whose applications for membership have been turned down naturally jumped to the conclusion that all sorts of things go on behind such jealously guarded doors. But they are quite wrong. My brother, who as one of the Assistant Commissioners of Scotland Yard would not feel inclined to wink at any irregularities, had supper with me there the other night.'

Dorene was scarcely listening to the latter part of his explanation. The name that he had let fall riveted her attention to the exclusion of everything else.

'What name did you say just now?' she asked.

'Name? Oh, you mean the Johnny who runs the show. His name is Mattioli — Andrea Mattioli. Needless to say, he hails from a sunnier clime than ours.'

'An Italian?'

'Presumably,' Terry shrugged carelessly. 'He seems to be a great friend of Professor Dangelli's. At least the old professor is a pretty regular visitor at 'The Laughing Mask'. But perhaps that doesn't stand for much,' he added as an

afterthought. 'The head cook-and-bottle-washer of a night club gets to know crowds of people — and some of them pretty queer fish. I saw Mattioli having a heart to heart confab with Rotheimer the other day. By the way, he used to be employed at the Pantheon Theatre when it first opened. Superintending the eats-and-drink department, apparently, for I saw him flitting about the refreshment bar at the back of the Dress Circle. That's the worst of modern evening clothes — you never can tell whether a fellow's a waiter, a theatre manager, or one of the general public.'

Dorene Grey nodded absently. Her mind was working rapidly. She could not get rid of the impression that this Andrea Mattioli was the man in whose house she had rented her flat, and the fact that he was on intimate terms with so many of her own by no means extensive circle of acquaintances struck her as being something more than a mere coincidence. If she had been willing to visit 'The Laughing Mask' before, now she was positively eager. Instinctively she had a

feeling that many little details, each isolated and trifling in itself, were on the point of fitting themselves together in an intelligible pattern.

The only outward sign to mark the entrance of the club was a small picture of a Greek comic mask painted on the upper panel of an otherwise plain green door wedged unobtrusively between a tailor's shop and a tobacconist's in a side street off Shaftesbury Avenue. The door swung open beneath Terry's hand, and Dorene found herself in a dark and narrow passage whose farther end was rendered even narrower by a construction not unlike the pay-box of a theatre. On the ledge before the window lay an open book, and in this Terry scribbled his name, afterwards handing the pen to Dorene.

'A trifling formality,' he explained with a smile.

Without glancing at the names, the girl seated inside the box pressed a lever with her foot, swinging open a door so narrow that only one person could enter at a time. Beyond this was a richly-carpeted

staircase leading downward.

A pair of bright crimson curtains, each having in its centre a laughing mask embroidered in gold thread, shrouded a wide archway at the foot of the stairs. The keystone of the arch was formed of an immense representation of the same symbol of Greek comedy moulded in plaster, and from its gaping mouth there proceeded a constant stream of roars of deep-throated laughter. On the curve of the arch was a motto picked out in letters of startling crimson: LAUGH AND THE WORLD LAUGHS WITH YOU.

Terry could himself scarcely refrain from adding the sound of his own merriment as he noted the half-startled glance which the girl cast upward.

'It's only a loud-speaker recording,' he said carelessly. 'Mattioli evidently believes that laughter is contagious. Maybe he studied psychology at the same school as Professor Dangelli. The professor is a great believer in the imitative instinct of the human biped!'

Terry drew aside one of the curtains as he spoke, and stood on one side to allow

141

Dorene to enter.

The place had originally been a basement belonging to the shop above, and probably used as a storage room or workshop. A lavish expenditure of money had effected a complete transformation. At first sight its exact size was difficult to judge, for by a skilful use of mirrors a fictitious effect of spaciousness was given to what were in reality blank walls.

Although almost every person, male and female, had cigarettes in their mouths, the clearness of the atmosphere was a tribute to the efficiency of the system of ventilation.

The scheme of decoration was vivid and startling in colour and absurdly grotesque in design. If a horde of demented artists, every one of them filled with insatiable futuristic yearnings, had been provided with pots of paint of the brightest possible hues, and let loose to give rein to their irresponsible imaginations on walls and ceiling, the resultant frescos could not have been more ludicrous and bizarre.

There were perhaps a hundred small

tables scattered about the place, some ranged round the walls, others half hidden in odd nooks and corners which suggested rather than actually afforded an atmosphere of privacy. In point of fact, anyone behind the little circular bar in the centre of the room could keep a watchful eye on every person present.

It was quickly apparent that Terry Hilton was well known to the habitués of the club. As he made his way up to the room he was forced to pause and return the greetings of almost every person whom he passed.

He found an unoccupied table at last and glanced quizzically across at Dorene.

'Do you still hanker after tea, or can I tempt you into indulging in a cocktail and sandwich?'

The girl's lips rippled in a smile as she shook her head.

'The general atmosphere of the place seems to indicate cocktails. But would the waiter be very shocked if I stick to my original choice?'

'You can't shock Francisco,' he told her. 'His brain is insulated against

anything short of a 50,000-volt electric current.'

Terry beckoned to the man and gave his order.

'See that old man sitting in the corner over there, drinking cider?' Terry said presently. 'When you're looking at him you're looking at the cleverest character actor in London. He specializes in Irish parts, but he can tackle anything from a Zulu chief to a Cockney dustman. I've seen him play both in one night.'

The man indicated, a tall, imposing figure with a mass of silvery white hair sweeping his coat collar, chanced to glance up at the moment. A smile of recognition lit up his thin, ascetic features as he caught Terry's eye, and he immediately rose and came across to the table where he and Dorene were seated.

'Hullo, Paddy,' Terry greeted the old man with the familiarity of an old acquaintance. 'How is the world using you?'

'Very scurvily, Mr. Hilton,' the Irishman answered with a shake of his venerable head. 'It's a disappointed and

sadly disillusioned man I am this night, sir.'

Terry's brows lifted in genuine surprise.

'I'm sorry to hear that — I thought you were well on the way to fame and fortune. I heard that you had gone into the film business.'

'I did, sir, to my sorrow and regret. Well, well,' he shrugged with theatrical deliberation, 'I suppose one cannot touch pitch and escape being defiled.'

'Defiled?' remonstrated the younger actor. 'Oh come, come!'

Paddy Doyle seated himself in the vacant chair by Terry's side and leaned his elbow on the table.

'When I said 'defiled' I spoke mildly, and when I said 'pitch' I did not use the first word which came into my mind,' he said with dignity. 'Had it not been for the presence of this charming young lady I might have used a stronger and more fitting term with which to express my opinion of films and the people who run them! Six months ago, sir, I was engaged by a director — whose name I will not

145

soil my lips by repeating — to play the part of Father O'Malley in *The Crossroads Of Crime*. I will not deny that it was a small part, but it was one of the most important in the piece. I kicked my heels at the studio for a week, waiting to do my stuff. And when it was all over, what do you think was the amount of remuneration that was handed to me?'

'I haven't the least idea,' Terry confessed.

'For playing an important part, they had the audacity to give me little more than a mere 'extra' gets for just walking on with the crowd!' cried the old man in a voice of tragedy. 'Was that fair? No, by Saint Patrick! And out of my paltry fee I had to pay ten percent to Rattenbury as his agent's fee.'

Terry leaned suddenly forward, a light of deeper interest in his eyes than had been awakened by the old actor's tale of woe.

'Rattenbury!' he exclaimed. 'Did you have your name on that man's books?'

'I did, sir; but that was the only engagement that he ever got me. Oh, I

know he was a scallywag,' Doyle went on. 'I just kept my name on his books because I was sorry for him, and I was sorrier still for his wife. I used to know her years ago, before she made the mistake of her life marrying him. She was in variety — I forget her particular line of business. She was a nice little woman, far too good for a skunk like him. He ill-treated her, too. Not that she ever complained — she wasn't that sort — but you know how these things get round in our profession. When last I heard of her she was living in a tumble-down cottage in a little Kentish village called Highspur Heath — '

Terry heard the girl's loud gasp of amazement and looked up quickly. Dorene Grey, white to the lips, was staring at the speaker with wide-open eyes.

'Highspur Heath — that is the place where I was living!' she cried in the voice of one who for the first time sees light breaking through the darkness. 'I know the woman you mean though she does not pass under the name of Mrs.

Rattenbury. Why, it was she who first showed me the advertisement in the paper and urged me to answer it in person! She also gave me contact details for my present lodgings. And she was the wife of the man who was murdered? The mystery seems to be getting deeper and deeper.'

Terry shook his head as he rose to his feet and motioned to the waiter to bring the check.

'On the contrary, Dorene, the mystery may be getting clearer,' he said cheerfully. 'The new facts may put the end of a thread into the hands of the C.I.D., and it remains to be seen where it will lead to.'

13

Dorene Grey was a young lady endowed with the average amount of sound, common sense, but she was not naturally of a suspicious turn of mind. It was only the following morning that her mind, refreshed with sleep, began dimly to glimpse a possibility that caused her first feeling of surprise to be tinged with misgiving.

She had taken the old lawyer entirely on trust. His outward aspect of respectability had been such that she had never dreamed of questioning his verbal statements. Now it was forced on her memory with disquieting insistence that those statements had not been backed up by documentary proof. He had produced a copy of her father's will, it is true, but he had himself admitted that such a copy could be obtained by anybody who made application at Somerset House and tendered the usual fees. What if this

self-styled solicitor were but another strand in the web of mystery and intrigue in which she had suddenly become enmeshed?

Dorene's breakfast that morning was a brief and hasty meal. It was but a few hundred yards from her flat to the Holborn Public Library, and shortly after that institution opened its doors she was eagerly turning the pages of the Post Office Directory, determined to find out whether such a firm had any real existence.

Cairncross and Beeding, Solicitors and Commissioners for Oaths, 98b, Gray's Inn, Holborn. She gave a sigh of relief as she read the line of close print. She had been half fearing that the portly, white-whiskered solicitor might prove as elusive as the mysterious Phantom of the Films.

The office of Messrs. Cairncross and Beeding was on the second floor of a building of mellow red brick, with a steep-pitched roof and windows of small leaded panes. A grave-faced clerk took her name, and almost directly afterwards she was ushered into the presence of the

head of the firm.

Mr. Cairncross was affability personified.

'Certainly, my dear Miss Grey,' he answered when she had stated her errand. 'Our firm will make you an immediate advance with the greatest pleasure in the world. How much do you require?'

The old solicitor glanced up, his pen poised over the open cheque book, and smiled as he saw the girl hesitate.

'Come, now, don't be afraid that you'll be asking too much. You are a very rich young lady now, remember. Will five hundred pounds be enough to go on with until — '

'Five hundred!' Dorene exclaimed quickly. 'Oh, I don't require nearly as much as that! Half that amount will be quite sufficient for the present — I should be scared to death carrying all that money about with me — especially after what happened last night.'

'And pray, what did happen last night?'

'I had my purse stolen, and your business card happened to be in it,' and in a few words Dorene gave him the gist of

her misadventure.

For an appreciable space Cairncross remained silently stroking his chin. His face had suddenly become grave. These signs of uneasiness did not escape the girl's observant eyes.

'You seem to attach considerable importance to the loss of your card,' she said. 'Surely you cannot suspect that that thief was aware that it was in my purse?'

The old man appeared to rouse himself from the reverie with an effort.

'Well, Miss Grey, that depends on who the thief was. If it was a mere chance encounter — ' He broke off with a shrug. 'I take it that the man who jostled against you was a stranger to you?'

'Quite.'

'Can you describe him?'

'Oh, yes. He was dressed — '

'It does not matter about his clothes,' interrupted the lawyer, 'at the best they are but a transient means of identification. His face?'

'I did not see his face on either occasion.'

'Either occasion? Then you had met him before?'

Dorene shook her head. 'No, after.'

'Where?' The word was jerked out with a harshness very different from the lawyer's normal, urbane tone.

'I caught a fleeting glimpse of him again as I was leaving 'The Laughing Mask'.'

The lawyer's lips tightened as he gave a grim nod.

'The theatrical night club, run by a certain Andrea Mattioli. I know it!'

It was the tone of voice rather than the actual words that made a startled look flash into Dorene's eyes.

'Do you know anything against Mr. Mattioli?' she asked quickly.

'I'm afraid I cannot answer that question definitely, Miss Grey. Many years of legal experience have given me a healthy respect for the law relating to slander — '

'But surely there is no harm in your telling me the truth?' cried the girl.

Walter Cairncross indulged in a twisted smile. 'My dear young lady, when you have reached my age you may perhaps

realize that telling the truth, otherwise than in a court of law, is a most dangerous practice. I cannot speak plainer than to advise you to give 'The Laughing Mask' a wide berth in future.'

'But if Mattioli were an undesirable person, surely the police would not allow him to run the club.'

'He is a mere paid servant — a kind of superior waiter. The licence is held by someone else, someone who is careful to keep in the background.'

A puzzled frown marred the smoothness of Dorene's forehead.

'Is it permissible for you to tell me the name of this mysterious person?' she asked a trifle coldly.

Mr. Cairncross appeared to debate the question in his own mind for a few seconds.

'Yes,' he said at length, 'I can see no objection to answering that question. The real owner of 'The Laughing Mask' is Professor Niccolo Dangelli.'

Dorene drew back as if she had been struck and the hot colour mounted to her cheeks.

'That man was one of my father's oldest and closest friends!' she cried. 'I've met him again recently, and he's offered me employment in his new film.'

'He *was* your father's friend,' the old man returned deliberately. 'He was *more* than your father's friend — he was his confidante. Miss Grey,' he sank his voice to an impressive whisper, 'Professor Dangelli is the only living man, outside official circles, who knows the nature of the terrible weapon which your father invented — the weapon that may change the destinies of nations — and — '

'Yes, yes?' The prompting words seemed dragged from her as the lawyer paused.

'*Professor Dangelli is the Phantom of the Films!*'

For an instant the revelation left her dumb. Then a contemptuous laugh issued from her white lips.

'I don't believe it! I cannot believe it!' she went on with a growing sense of conviction. 'You have deceived yourself, Mr. Cairncross, or somebody has deceived you. If you have proof of what you say,

why do you not denounce him to the police?'

The lawyer shook his head sadly and made a little helpless gesture with his hands.

'I have no proof that would be admitted in a court of law,' he confessed. 'Yet in my own mind I am certain that I am not mistaken. On the occasion when I met the professor at your father's house, he himself brought up and outlined just such another plan whereby a reign of terror could be created by a criminal who hid his identity behind a film. I thought he was merely jesting at the time, but now I know that he was in deadly earnest. Down to the smallest detail, the procedure that Dangelli then sketched out was that which has been adopted by the fantastic being who calls himself the Phantom.'

The girl threw back her head with a gesture of fierce denial.

'Well may you say that you have no proof!' Icy mockery rang through her voice. 'It passes my understanding how you, a lawyer, a man who should know

the meaning of the word 'evidence', can make such a charge on the strength of such a flimsy piece of gossip uttered over a dinner table. A murderer must have a motive for his crimes. What motive had Dangelli? Answer me that. What motive had he?'

'None!'

'Ah, then — '

Mr. Cairncross held up his hands with a slow, ominous motion that made her cry of triumph die on her lips.

'A madman needs no motive,' he said with a strange, grim smile, 'and Professor Dangelli is mad!'

Then his lips closed like a vice as he handed the cheque to Dorene and bowed her to the door.

14

As Dorene Grey descended the narrow oak staircase and emerged from the lawyer's office her mind was in a state of excited bewilderment, which almost made connected thought impossible.

Dangelli the Phantom? Dangelli insane? She found herself on the point of laughing aloud at the absurdity of the ideas. Had not the professor deliberately thrust himself before the notice of the police? Had he not drawn attention to himself by writing a film drama in which he intended to depict the solution of the grotesque mystery that had set all England talking and wondering? Had he not been her father's oldest and closest friend? Queer and eccentric he might be; one who dabbled in the detection of cunning criminals and unravelled intricate crime tangles with the same skill, patience and enthusiasm as the keen angler or ardent hunter pursues his

favourite sport. That frail old man guilty of a murder? Sooner than credit that she would have suspected one of the high officials of Scotland Yard itself to be the guilty man!

She cashed the open cheque at the nearest branch of the bank whose name it bore, and as she left the building almost the first person she encountered was the very man who occupied her thoughts.

'Fortune is kind to me this morning,' Professor Dangelli bent over her hand with an exaggerated old-world courtesy that made the bystanders stare. 'You are the young lady whom I most desired to meet.'

'Indeed Professor? Then it is a double coincidence. I, too, was anxious to have a little talk with you. I have just come from an interview with a solicitor named Walter Cairncross.'

Somewhat to her surprise, he gave a smile of ready recognition at the mention of the name.

'I know that gentleman. I met him at your father's house, and probably the

good Walter has not forgotten the occasion. He is a very shrewd man, is Walter — ' he paused and caressed his short beard — 'I wonder how far his shrewdness will carry him — in the right direction?'

Dangelli crooked his finger to the driver of a passing taxi, and almost before the girl was aware of the fact she found herself seated at his side and being borne rapidly westward.

'Where are we going?' she asked when the taxi had entered Oxford Street.

'We are going to transact a little business, you and I.'

The girl's brows flickered upward.

'Important business?' she asked, and the old professor nodded gravely

'Business of the utmost importance that the feminine mind can conceive.' His eyes twinkled beneath their shaggy brows. 'We are about to look at the shops.'

'The shops?' she repeated, the look of bewilderment deepening in her eyes. 'What kind of shops?'

Professor Dangelli indulged in an elaborate shrug.

'Oh milliners and drapers and dress-makers, and those shops which purvey the dainty little articles of feminine adornment too numerous to be grasped by the uninitiated male. I confess my limitations, you perceive, Miss Grey, and that is where I require your help. I am about to choose the outward embellishments of the heroine in my coming film drama.'

'But I understood that I was to play that part,' she exclaimed.

'Exactly. We are about to choose your own costume.'

Dorene uttered a little cry of protest.

'But you have been so kind already in offering me the leading part. I really could not allow — '

He silenced her with a gentle, kindly wave of his hand.

'Dorene, I am old enough to be your father,' he said with an earnestness that was almost pathetic. 'An old man has his whims and fancies — and also, maybe, his privileges. Please do not deny me mine. Were I a younger man my offer would be an insult. Were I not vitally interested in

this film, it might be still be resented. But, by the friendship that once existed between your father and myself, I assure you that I am not acting as I am without good and sufficient reason. The clothes themselves shall be entirely of your own choosing — I should indeed be rash if I attempted to dicate to a young lady as to what did and what did not suit her own particular type of beauty. But I wish to give instructions to those responsible for the — er — the fashioning of the various garment, so that they may be useful as well as ornamental. Please don't ask me explain. Please trust me,' he continued in a tone of deep sincerity. 'Believe me, both you and — unless I am very much mistaken — a certain good-looking young actor will have reason to bless what must now appear like the unwarrantable interference of an old fool with matters which do not concern him.'

At any other time Dorene might have smiled, but now her eyes felt unaccountably moist as she mutely nodded her head.

'Then we can regard that as settled,

eh?' Dangelli reached for the speaking tube and ordered the driver to stop. 'Here we are in the very midst of the shopping centre. Lead me where you will, young lady, for this is decidedly an occasion when the feminine hand should be at the helm. And now let us see what treasures we can discover behind the miles of shop windows by which we are surrounded.'

The average member of the male sex is apt to find a mannequin parade a somewhat boring function. Dangelli, however, was as interested as a child with a new toy. But, perhaps realizing that he was treading on strange and dangerous ground, he was very sparing with his suggestions — a fact for which Dorene was duly grateful. He contented himself with giving one little word of caution.

'Don't let your judgment be led away by pretty colours my dear,' he warned her. 'And especially avoid yellow and red. They will come out black in the film, you know, and the heroine is not supposed to be mourning.'

Dorene took the timely hint to heart, and concentrated her attention on the

outline and form of the models paraded for her inspection. For the most part the professor merely signified his approval with a smiling nod as she made her choice but when it came to deciding on the long, fur-trimmed coat, he for the first time evinced decided opinions as to a suitable style.

'I — er — fancy these styles are a trifle tight-fitting,' he said to the sales-lady after about a dozen beautiful but supercilious damsels had wafted themselves across his range of vision. 'I thought that something — er — a trifle roomier — '

'But the shaped coats are the latest mode,' protested the black-gowned mistress of the ceremonies. 'And modom has such an exquisite figure!'

It was but the usual stock phrase of subtle flattery, but in the present instance it happened to be no more than the exact truth. But Dangelli, hitherto so pliant in his opinions, now became stubborn indeed.

'Nevertheless, I think a little straighter model would be advisable,' he insisted, regardless of the sales-lady's scorn at such

heresy towards the sacred tenets of the prevailing fashion.

At that the sales-lady diplomatically conceded the point.

'Doubtless modom can explain her particular requirements to the fitter when that coat is fitted?'

'*I* will explain the requirements when it is fitted,' snapped Dangelli.

The lady in the black gown became frozenly polite.

'Very good, sir. And the cloth? And the trimming?'

'I leave that to modom,' grinned the professor.

In the end Dorene's choice fell on a design of dove-grey cloth with a collar of some magnificent silver fox skins that were brought out for her inspection. As Dangelli went to the desk to pay the deposit he drew the manageress aside.

'I would like a few words with the foreman of your workroom, if you have no objection.'

The manageress hesitated. 'It is unusual — '

'I am an unusual man,' broke in

Dangelli impatiently. 'If there is any extra charge, put it on the bill.'

A few moments later he was in conversation with a stout, dark-haired man who bore visible signs of his trade in the numerous ends of white cotton which clung to his clothing. When Dangelli had finished speaking he had reduced the wielder of the needle to a condition of gasping stupefaction. Never in the course of his thirty years' experience of the trade had Mr. Abrahams received such strange instructions regarding the making of a lady's coat.

15

Mr. Cyril Boyd-Pennington, architect and surveyor, was a man of very methodical business habits. At half-past nine every weekday morning he would unlock the door of his first-floor suite of offices at Number 1, Little Cambridge Street, with an unvarying regularity which made the other tenants of the block declare that they might set their clocks by the sound of his latchkey and not find them more than a few seconds out of Greenwich Mean Time. Before settling down at his drawing-board, it was Mr. Boyd-Pennington's custom to go through his correspondence. Usually this took but a very few minutes, for his practice was by no means extensive. On that particular morning his mail consisted of a single letter bearing a large black seal on which was impressed a heralding device consisting of a lofty, battlemented tower; beneath it was a motto: *Beccati questo*.

'H'mph — Italian?' muttered Boyd-Pennington, for a working knowledge of that language was one of the accomplishments of the plump little architect.

There was a thoughtful smile on his fleshy lips as he took a pair of scissors and carefully slit the top of the envelope, leaving the seal intact. It seemed as if the sight of the Italian motto had flashed an instinctive warning to his brain.

Inside was a sheet of thick, parchment notepaper, and on it a few lines written in a hand so neat as to be almost effeminate:

Dear sir: (it ran) I wish very particularly to consult you regarding a commission of a somewhat unusual nature. I will call at your office at ten o'clock on the morning you receive this letter. Please phone me if this is not convenient. (Here followed a number on the Richmond Exchange).

For a long while the architect remained gazing at the neat signature, *Niccolo Dangelli*. The name conveyed nothing to Cyril Boyd-Pennington's mind. The writer was an entire stranger to him.

Boyd-Pennington read the letter for the

third time before laying it face upward on the pad before him. From a box on the desk he took a cigar, long and thin, having a straw running through its centre. Lighting it he lay back in his swivel chair, watching through narrowed lips the spirals of smoke as they wreathed upwards to the somewhat dingy ceiling. Once his hand strayed towards the telephone receiver on the desk. But even as he made the movement the little clock on the mantelpiece chimed the three-quarters. A quarter to ten! — apparently the unknown Dangelli had so timed his intended visit that even a phone call to his residence would not reach him in time for it to be postponed or refused. Was it by accident or by deliberate design that this letter making the appointment had been received when he was already well on his way to the architect's office?

Mr. Boyd-Pennington shrugged his heavy shoulders and left the question undecided. Rising to his feet, he thrust his hands deep into his trouser pockets and strolled to the window overlooking the street. Still puffing slowly at his cigar, he

allowed his gaze to travel across the wide intervening space and rest on the lane of windows of the large block of offices whose front elevation faced the busy main thoroughfare of New Cambridge Street. One window bore a printed notice, OFFICE TO LET, and the little architect's cherubic features grew serious as he mechanically read the sign. The last occupier's tenancy of those premises had been terminated with grim and tragic abruptness. In that room Amos Rattenbury had died with a dagger in his heart.

'Gad!' Boyd-Pennington exclaimed with sudden and hearty conviction. 'I'm not a rich man, but I'd give every penny I possess to know the real identity of the Phantom of the Films! He must be a cunning devil, or he wouldn't have eluded the police for so long. I wonder if they'll ever catch him? And I wonder if they'll ever find out what his real name is?'

His train of thought snapped abruptly as a magnificent Daimler swept round the corner and glided to a standstill at the kerb immediately below the window.

Craning his neck, Boyd-Pennington caught a foreshortened glimpse of a tall grey-haired stranger as he alighted and entered the building.

Boyd-Pennington immediately drew back from the window and, pausing only to hurl his half-smoked cigar into the fireplace, seated himself at his desk and affected to be immersed in the study of some half-completed plans.

'Come in,' he said presently in answer to the expected knock.

He glanced round with a preoccupied air as his visitor entered. For an instant the bovine eyes behind the horn-rimmed spectacles were unusually keen and searching as he examined the bearded face with one swift glance. It confirmed his previous impression. The man was a complete stranger to him.

'Signor Niccolo Dangelli?'

The stranger bowed.

'That is my name, sir,' he said gravely, 'and by your use of it I perceive that it is needless for me to ask if you received my letter. But why do you prefix it with 'Signor'?'

The little architect permitted himself to smile.

'Well, sir, your name has a distinctly Italian sound. When in addition, I saw that your handwriting betrayed unmistakable Latin characteristics, I naturally assumed that the title would not be out of place.'

Professor Dangelli smiled in his turn as he sniffed the smoke-laden air.

'I perceive that you have the detective instinct strongly developed, Mr. Boyd-Pennington. I suppose that if I had chanced to share your own partiality for Italian cigars your chain of evidence would have been complete?'

The architect's clean-shaven features went a slightly deeper red. He rather prided himself on his detective abilities, and the implied rebuke was quite unexpected.

'I'm sorry if I was wrong — '

Dangelli brushed aside the stammered apology with a smiling wave of his slender hand.

'You were not wholly wrong, neither were you quite right. It is true that I come

172

from an old Tuscan family — an ancestor of mine won that crest and motto by his defence of the Castello di Chiusi in the Thirteenth Century. But it is many years since I lived in Italy, and I prefer to be known as just plain 'Mr.' I find that the English prefix makes me appear less strange and — er — sinister in the eyes of people who meet me for the first time.'

'Quite so, *Mister* Dangelli,' the other hastened to agree. 'Perhaps it is only natural. Taking us on the whole, sir, we are apt to be somewhat insular.'

Professor Dangelli lifted his narrow shoulders in a protest shrug.

'Nay, you do yourself an injustice, sir,' he declared warmly. 'A man who has a taste for the cigars of my native land, and who recognizes Italian handwriting at a glance, must possess a mind above all petty national prejudices. Doubtless you have travelled very extensively in Italy?'

'No.'

Dangelli's eyebrows twitched upward at the curt disclaimer.

'No?' he repeated in a tone that seemed to imply that he had not heard aright.

'You mean to say that you have never visited that most beautiful country?'

'Never!' Boyd-Pennington spoke very slow and distinct. 'The only occasion that I visited the Continent was when I went to France — and that wasn't a pleasure trip,' he added grimly.

The professor's keen eyes strayed toward the framed photo of a round-faced man in the uniform of a British officer, which hung over the mantelpiece.

'I see,' he said, nodding sagaciously. 'You went at the call of duty, is it not so? Ah, a terrible war, sir, a terrible war! The sufferings of the infantry in the trenches — '

'I served in the Artillery,' the other interrupted shortly. With an impatient movement he turned and searched among the papers that littered the top of his desk. 'I see by your letter that you wish to consult me regarding a commission of a somewhat unusual nature, Mr. Dangelli?'

It was impossible for the most obtuse person to mistake the direct hint. Instantly Dangelli was all apologies.

'A thousand pardons, my dear Mr.

Boyd-Pennington. I fear that my insatiable appetite for idle gossip has led me far from the subject that brought me here. To business, then.' He seated himself in the chair on the further side of the desk and went on briskly: 'I am about to produce a film — and I wished to know if you would undertake to draw up the plans and generally supervise the architectural setting for some of the scenes in it. Are you willing to undertake this description of work?'

Boyd-Pennington hesitated.

'I fear that you have come to the wrong man, sir,' he answered after an appreciable pause. 'I cannot claim to be an experienced scenic designer — '

'All that I require you to do is to construct a replica of an existing building, and your task will be rendered all the easier by the fact that you have already surveyed the premises and drawn out a scale plan quite recently.'

'Indeed?' The architect's features took on an expression of blank surprise. 'It may assist my memory if you tell me who commissioned the work.'

'Scotland Yard,' was the prompt reply. 'The principal scene of my film is laid in the first-floor office immediately opposite to your own window,' and Dangelli pointed to the house across the road.

Mr. Boyd-Pennington allowed his hands to fall on the desk as he stared at his client in something approaching stupefaction.

'Rattenbury's office?' he cried incredulously. 'The place where the murder was committed?'

'Exactly,' smiled the imperturbable Dangelli.

'But — a film drama? — acted in a facsimile for the actual room?'

'And with the same people playing — so far as circumstance permit — the same parts as they played in the real life tragedy,' supplemented the other calmly. 'It ought to make a sensation, eh?'

'A sensation? Good heavens — !'

'Especially as I shall be careful to advertise that the one-and-only, authentic Phantom of the Films will appear in the film in person and explain in detail how the murder was committed.'

At the words a veil seemed to drop over Boyd-Pennington's bulging eyes.

'You will promise that?' he asked slowly. 'You know who the Phantom is?' Dangelli nodded.

'And you can induce him to play his part in your film?' resumed Boyd-Pennington.

Professor Dangelli's eyelids flickered, but he merely raised his shoulders indifferently as though weary at the persistent questioning.

'The Phantom of the Films will give a complete exposé of the mystery which is puzzling all England,' he returned in a tone of quiet decision. 'That is the whole point of my intended film.'

The assurance seemed to sweep the last vestiges of hesitation from the architect's mind.

'Then you may count on my co-operation so far as the setting of the scene is concerned,' he said.

Dangelli nodded and his right hand strayed towards the inner pocket of his coat. 'As to the question of terms — '

'That can wait. My work will be a

labour of love so long as I am assured that it will assist to bring that dastardly murderer to justice!' Boyd-Pennington declared with an eagerness that was quite unexpected. 'I merely stipulate one condition.'

'And that is — '

'That I may be allowed to be there when the final scenes of the film are shot.'

Professor Dangelli inclined his head and a bleak smile played about his bearded lips.

'Agreed,' he said as he prepared to take his leave. 'Rest content, Mr. Boyd-Pennington. You shall be in at the death.'

The chauffeur sprang down to open the door of the Daimler as Professor Dangelli emerged into the street, but the old man shook his head.

'I have a little walking to do, Vincenzo,' he said in the harsh Tuscan dialect. 'Pick me up in twenty minutes' time outside the British Museum.'

Turning on his heel, Dangelli strode briskly across the main thoroughfare and plunged into the narrow alley, which runs beside the Tube station. Five minutes

later he was ringing at the street door of Dorene Grey's flat.

The florid-faced landlady gave him a stare in which fear and servility were curiously blended.

'Miss Grey is not at 'ome,' she said in answer to his inquiry.

Professor Dangelli nodded his head and waited. The brows that arched above his glittering eyes were mutely demanding further details.

'She went out about an hour ago,' Mrs. Mattioli added.

'Alone?' The question came with the sharpness of a pistol shot and into the professor's eyes there flashed a queer look which only died as the woman shook her head.

'Some feller called for her in a car — a little two-seater.'

'Was the man young, handsome, clean-shaven?' Dangelli rapped out, and again the woman nodded.

'You've said it, guv'nor,' she agreed.

Professor Dangelli smiled with the air of one whose mind is relieved.

'It is well,' he murmured softly, scarcely

above his breath. 'And was Miss Grey wearing her new coat?' he went on blandly.

'The grey one with the fur collar and cuffs? Yes, she was wearing it.'

'Again it is well,' murmured the old man; then, raising his soft felt hat with courtly gesture: 'I have the honour to wish madame 'Good-day'.'

Mrs. Mattioli seemed taken aback at his sudden termination of the interview.

' 'Old on a minute, sir,' she breathed in an urgent whisper. 'Did yer get the message that I — '

'Once more I have the honour to wish madame 'Good-day',' he repeated firmly. Still smiling his inscrutable smile, the professor replaced his hat and strode quickly in the direction of his waiting car.

16

At the same time as the professor was evincing such a close interest in Dorene Grey's whereabouts, the girl herself was seated by the side of Terry Hilton in a powerful little two-seater that was swiftly breasting the steep gradient of Shooter's Hill, in the Kentish outskirts of London.

The previous afternoon Terry had gone to great pains to seek out his brother at his office at Scotland Yard to discuss the Rattenbury case. Sir Digby referred ruefully to the 'red herring' detention of the architect Boyd-Pennington, but Terry wasn't greatly interested. Excitedly, he explained to his brother in detail that Amos Rattenbury's widow was living under an assumed name at Highspur Heath, and that she had been the direct means of introducing to Dorene's notice Rattenbury's advertisement. To his disappointment, however, he found Digby strangely apathetic.

'As a friendly admirer of Miss Grey I am interested in your description of how she came to launch into her theatrical career,' the Assistant Commissioner informed him with a smile, 'but officially your news leaves me cold. I am betraying no secret when I say that we have eliminated Miss Grey from the list of suspects.'

'I should think so indeed!' Terry had cried indignantly. 'Why, sooner than suspect that dear girl I would suspect — '

'Me?' queried Digby with a twisted smile as his brother paused. 'No, old lad, we're too hot on the main trail to be interested in side-tracks just now. The main trail, I hardly need explain, leads to the Phantom of the Films.'

'Then I can only wish you good hunting,' the younger man snorted with something like contempt. 'I give you fair warning that Dorene and I are going to do some investigating on our own — down in Kent.'

Sir Digby shrugged as he turned to the papers on his desk.

'I never throw cold water on the enthusiasm of youth,' he replied sententiously.

'So it only remains for me to return your good wishes. Good hunting, old son, and I hope you both enjoy the trip.'

Terry had taken him at his word; and now, as he glanced at the beautiful profile of the girl's flushed face, he found it in his heart to bless the official policy that had made the trip possible.

The day was warm and sunny, with scarcely a breath of wind, and the countryside looked its best. The tall trees that lined the hill still flaunted summer's verdant insignia on their leafy banners, as though they were loth to assume the drab livery of autumn. The crest of the hill past, there opened before them a wide and extensive prospect of fields, studded here and there with the roof of some farmhouse or villa, dappled with bronze-green and harvest gold; until, miles and miles distant, all detail was lost in the shimmering blue haze of the distant horizon.

On their right hand, so dim that it might have escaped notice but for the reflection of the sun on its waters, the broad Thames lay like a ribbon of

burnished metal as it wound its sinuous path to the far-off sea.

'Another four miles,' informed the girl, as the car began its downward swoop on the further slope of the hill. 'And a straight, downhill road half the way.'

'Oh, I'm in no hurry,' laughed Terry. He would have been twice as pleased if they had double that distance to traverse before they reached their destination.

'It's been a delightful run,' Dorene agreed. 'I like your car.'

With difficulty Terry repressed a desire to tell her that the car, together with everything else he possessed, was entirely at her disposal.

'Not a bad little bus,' he said instead. 'Her engine is half as big again as that of the usual car of the same type. I've been holding her in all the way down. You ought to see her streak when I really lean on the pedal.'

'I think I'll choose a car of the same make when — '

She broke off, and Terry looked at her curiously.

'When your ship comes home?' he

laughingly completed the sentence.

'That's it.' Her answering laugh was vibrant with relief. Thoughtlessly she had been on the point of revealing the huge legacy that had enabled her to indulge in such luxuries. 'We turn off here,' she added as they approached a side road branching to the right. 'I'm quite willing to take your word for the streaking abilities of your car, Terry, so you can take your foot off the accelerator pedal. These winding lanes are scarcely suited for a speed test.'

'Why not keep to the main road?'

Dorene hesitated a second.

'I don't want to advertise my visit to Highspur Heath — I'm very well known in the village. If we make a circuit, we can approach the cottage where Rattenbury's widow lives without passing through the main street of the village. By the way, I have always known that lady as Mrs. Peters.'

'Another alias? Well, the Rotheimer clan certainly seem to have a craze for changing their names. Maybe they found it very necessary now and then!'

The girl nodded thoughtfully and relapsed into silence.

When she spoke again it was to introduce a totally different topic of conversation.

'You haven't said how you liked my new coat, Terry.'

The young actor flashed the briefest of glances at the garment in question, then returned his gaze to the road ahead.

'It's very nice. You look adorable in it.'

'Really?' She smiled mischievously. 'Professor Dangelli will be flattered when I tell him that you approve of his taste.'

'Eh?' he jerked out in amazement. 'Dangelli? What has that fellow got to do with it?'

'He chose it.' Dorene's smile deepened as she saw his eyebrows go up, and she added deliberately: 'He paid for it, too.'

Terry's raised brows settled into a fierce frown.

'Very kind of him, I'm sure,' he muttered savagely. 'He seems to take a great interest in the matter of your attire.'

'He does,' she agreed with provocative

frankness. 'He gave me the hat I'm wearing.'

Terry drew a long breath and his face grew black as thunder. Dorene, watching him beneath her long lashes, felt her heart give a mad leap of joy as she noted these outward signs of jealousy.

'I think it's rotten!' he ground out fiercely.

'My hat — rotten?'

'No — the idea of your accepting presents like that.' He paused a moment to control his voice, and when he spoke again it held a note of tender earnestness that caused the girl to sit back in the cushioned seat, flushed and trembling, her eyes filled with a wistful wonder as though she had found something so precious that she doubted its reality. 'I love you, Dorene. It's been like a new world to me since I've known you. Looking back, I can't think how I've lived through all the years without you. If I were to lose you now — ' He broke off and his voice resumed its former tone: 'How long has this old fool been taking an interest in your clothes?'

187

'Ever since I signed the contract to appear in his film.' Her lips rippled back in a laugh. 'Dangelli is very anxious that I shall 'dress the part' according to his own ideas, that's all. I am to wear this costume in the big scene at the end of his play.'

'Then why wear it now?' he asked.

The girl shrugged as she shook her head.

'That was Dangelli's idea. He made me promise that I would wear this coat for ordinary occasions until the film was produced. He had been so kind and considerate that I couldn't very well refuse such a trifling request, could I?'

'Well, no,' Terry admitted, though somewhat dubiously. 'It seems a queer idea.'

He turned his head and examined the dove-grey coat with closer attention than he had hitherto exhibited.

'Do you trust this Dangelli?' he asked with startling abruptness.

Her eyes widened slightly.

'Why, of course! He was my father's dearest friend. I would trust him with my life.'

He bent his head and looked straight into her eyes. 'Would you trust *me* with it, Dorene?' he asked in a voice that trembled slightly.

'That question seems a trifle superfluous, Terry,' she answered lightly. 'I've been trusting my life to you for the last ten minutes, seeing that I've been sitting in a car which you are evidently trying to drive blindfold. You've taken three sharp corners with scarcely a glance at the road ahead.'

'I was admiring Dangelli's taste in ladies' coats,' said Terry mendaciously. 'I can't claim to be such a sartorial expert as he seems to be, but it appears just an ordinary coat to me. Is there anything unusual about it?'

Dorene hesitated and shifted the soft grey fur slightly off her shoulders.

'It seems a trifle warm and heavy for such a thin material,' she admitted with a puzzled air. 'I would not have worn it today if I had not given my promise to the old professor.'

'Heavy?' Terry's sly grin showed that the cloud of jealousy had not quite lifted

from his mind. 'Perhaps it's lined with sovereigns? I've heard that the old boy is enormously rich.'

'There is one thing more precious than riches, Terry,' she quoted solemnly, and her hearer grinned sardonically.

'Did you get that pearl of wisdom out of a copy-book of moral maxims?'

She shook her head.

'I got it out of the Book of Experience. I have had both things given to me lately, and I know which brings the greater happiness.' It was not until some time later that he understood the hidden meaning of the little smile which accompanied her words.

A turn of the narrow road brought them into sight of their destination.

Orchard Cottage stood well back from the road in a little patch of ground that bore signs of industrious cultivation. A few minutes' walking along a deeply-rutted lane brought them to the front of the house. Dorene pushed the gate and knocked on the shabby, sun-blistered green door. It opened with a startling suddenness that suggested a hand

already on the latch.

'Jarvis!' gasped the girl.

Instead of Mrs. Peters, the open doorway framed a burly figure in the uniform of a police constable.

'Jarvis it is, Miss Grey,' the man responded with a nod of instant recognition. 'What may you be wanting here, miss?'

'I called to see Mrs. Peters,' replied the wondering girl. 'Is she at home?'

The constable shook his head slowly. 'No, miss. I be in charge here until further orders.'

'But where is Mrs. Peters? Is she ill?'

'No, miss, not exactly what you could call ill.' The man's voice took on a sympathetic tone. 'If you were very friendly with the lady you'd better be prepared for a shock. Mrs. Peters died last night.'

Dorene Grey gave a gasp of surprise.

'Last night?' she echoed. 'She must have died suddenly?'

'Very suddenly. She committed suicide last night by stabbing herself to the heart.'

Terry stepped forward, his mind filled

with sudden suspicion.

'Suicide, you say?' he cried with unthinking impulsiveness. 'How can you be sure that it was suicide?'

P.C. Jarvis looked somewhat sheepish as he shrugged his broad shoulders. 'Well, sir, maybe that ain't for the likes of me to say. But 'tis certain sure that she was found in the middle of that patch of ground over there. It's newly turned soil, as you can see for yourself, and soft enough to take the lightest footprint. And the only traces we could find were the footprints of the woman herself.'

Terry turned and his eyes met Dorene's horrified gaze. In the mute message of the girl's eyes he read the same ominous presentiment that was hammering at his own brain.

The Phantom was at work again!

17

P.C. Jarvis noticed the girl's emotion, though he was far from suspecting the real reason for it.

'I dare say this has come as a bit of a shock, Miss Grey,' he said, glancing sympathetically at her bloodless features. 'Would you like to come inside for a bit and sit down?'

He stood aside from the door with a gesture of invitation, but Dorene recoiled.

'Is she — is the — ?'

Jarvis was quick to guess the half-spoken question.

'Oh, it's all right, miss,' he assured her. 'The poor lady has been removed to the mortuary.'

The little room, half kitchen, half living room, struck cold and chill after the bright sunshine outside. Scattered about were pathetic reminders of the woman whose life had been so suddenly cut short. The ashes lay cold and dead on the

hearth; a work basket stood on a small table and beside it was an unfinished piece of knitting. Noting these details, Terry Hilton was more convinced than ever that when the woman had last quitted that room she had had not the slightest inkling of her approaching fate. For the present, however, he determined to keep his suspicions to himself until he had an opportunity of communicating with his brother at Scotland Yard. Even in that room of tragic associations he could not help feeling a little thrill of satisfaction as he mentally pictured Digby's surprise when he informed him of the tragic termination of the trail which he had disdained to follow.

P.C. Jarvis was able to give first-hand details of the finding of the body, for he had himself seen it lying in the garden when he made his usual perambulation just before dusk the previous evening. He judged that the woman had then been dead for several hours, and the doctor whom he summoned confirmed his estimate. He was positive that there were no signs of other footprints near the body,

and his theory of the tragedy was a simple one.

'I dare say the poor woman had her troubles,' he summed up the situation to his own satisfaction. 'She was a queer person, by all accounts. Lived alone and scarcely spoke to a soul since she came to live here. I suppose you don't happen to know where we can find any of her relations?'

Dorene caught Terry's warning glance and shook her head.

'I believe she was a widow,' she temporized.

'Ah, well, I suppose she had her troubles, poor soul,' the policeman repeated with a wise shake of his head. 'Even in a village like this it's true enough that one half of the world doesn't know how the other half lives — '

'Or dies!' Terry added grimly.

'Very true, sir,' Jarvis agreed mechanically though he did not appreciate the full significance of the young man's words. 'Well, good morning, Miss Grey. Good morning, sir, and thank you.'

Terry performed a little sleight of hand,

and a rustling piece of engraved paper changed owners. Once out of sight from the cottage window, he turned excitedly to Dorene.

'This is where your local knowledge comes in useful, my dear. I want the nearest telephone, and I want it mighty badly. Let me get a connection and breathe six words, and Scotland Yard will be buzzing like an overturned beehive!'

'Telephone?' She repeated the word with something like dismay, her brows wrinkled in concentrated thought. Suddenly her face brightened. 'There are no public call-boxes here, but Dr. Howard has a phone. He's my father's successor and he lives in my old home. Come along!'

They set off at a rapid pace and some ten minutes later Dorene was breathlessly explaining to an elderly, grave-faced doctor the urgency of the occasion. Without wasting words, Dr. Howard conducted the young actor to his study and intimated that the phone was entirely at his disposal.

Not until the doctor had quitted the

room did Terry lift the receiver.

A few seconds served for him to electrify the Assistant Commissioner with the news of the fresh development. It was a very self-satisfied young man who hung up the receiver and went in search of the master of the house.

He found him in animated conversation with Dorene.

'I was very pleased indeed to see this young lady today,' he said, turning to Terry. 'I would have written to her to call here had I known her address. I have a little surprise awaiting her.'

'A surprise for me?' echoed Dorene.

'Yes. You remember that somewhat antique writing bureau which I took over with the rest of the furniture when I entered into possession here?'

'It belonged to my mother,' the girl said in a low voice.

'The other day I sent it to a firm of restorers to have a few small repairs effected,' resumed Dr. Howard. 'The workmen found a secret drawer, so cunningly concealed that it had escaped my notice — and also, I presume, yours

too. For it contained something which I am sure you did not know was there.'

The grey-haired doctor paused and a smile crossed his face as he noted the girl's eager expression.

'I trust I have not raised false hopes of the 'something' in question being hidden treasure, Miss Grey. Nothing so romantic or so desirable as that, unfortunately. Of course, I have not examined it in detail, but the find appears merely to consist of a bundle of letters, tied with a faded pink ribbon, and a few old photographs. Valueless in themselves though they may be, doubtless you, as the sole surviving member of your family, will prize them for the sentimental associations that may cling to them. At all events I am pleased to be the indirect means of restoring them to their rightful owner.'

With a little ceremonious bow he handed to Dorene the articles in question. A sad smile, wistful with tender memories, rose to her lips as she looked at the faded photographs.

'Yes, they belonged to my mother.' She handed to Terry a photo of an officer

wearing a gun badge on his cap and the three stars of a British captain on his shoulder straps. 'That was her only brother. It was taken just before he sailed with his battery for Italy.'

'Your uncle?' Terry asked. 'So you are not quite alone in the world after all?'

The girl shook her head.

'He was attached to the Second Army, and he was shot by a sniper while he and a brother officer were trying to locate a Trench Mortar Battery in the Vippacco Valley, near San Gabriele.'

Terry glanced again at the photograph. Written on the margin of the mount, in shaky characters, was; 'Captain Cyril Boyd-Pennington. Died for his Country, September 8th, 1943.'

Terry stared and remained standing with the photograph in his hand, his face like a mask of carved stone, his eyes veiled in thought.

Boyd-Pennington!

The name set a chord of memory vibrating in the dim recesses of his mind like a harp-string touched by a practised hand. Somewhere — recently — under

circumstances connected with the mysterious crime — he had heard that name before!

But when — and where? Terry could only shake his head helplessly. The name had conveyed nothing to him at the time; it had, in fact, produced no deeper impression on his memory than any of the casual names that are heard only to be completely forgotten.

Then, all unbidden, other names — names that he knew well — flashed into his mental view and ranged themselves by the side of the shadowy and elusive Boyd-Pennington.

'Boyd-Pennington . . . Italy . . . Niccolo Dangelli . . . Mattioli . . . Vippacco Valley . . . San Gabriele . . . Italy . . . Boyd-Pennington!' Always the vicious circle of his harassed thoughts came back to Cyril Boyd-Pennington. But the man was dead — killed in action.

The eyes of Terry Hilton narrowed and his lips set in a smile of grim triumph. He had heard the man's name mentioned much more recently than that date, and he certainly had not been spoken of as

one that was dead!

Still holding the photograph, he looked up at Dorene with a sudden question:

'May I keep this for a few hours?'

'Certainly, if you wish to,' was her wondering answer. 'But I must confess that I cannot understand your sudden interest in the man who, had he lived, would be my nearest relative.'

'Did Dangelli know this uncle of yours?' Terry asked.

'He knew of him, of course. But I am practically certain that they never met. Uncle Cyril very seldom visited us; there was an estrangement between my father and his brother-in-law. I'm afraid Cyril was rather wild in his younger days, before he settled down and became an articled pupil to an eminent architect.'

With difficulty Terry repressed a shout of joy as he thrust the photo into his pocket. Architect! The word burnt a definite idea, a definite memory, into his consciousness.

Cyril Boyd-Pennington was the man who had been arrested and afterwards released on the night when the mysterious

burglar wrecked the safe in Rattenbury's office. His place of business was less than a hundred yards from the spot where the murder was committed.

By the light that suddenly dawned in his brain, Terry Hilton thought he saw one possible answer to the riddle of the Phantom.

18

It was nearly midday when Professor Dangelli reached his home after his interview with the architect and his unsuccessful attempt to see Dorene Grey. Admitting himself with his latchkey, he proceeded at once to his study and rang the bell.

'I shall not require any lunch today, Mapes,' he said when the butler made his appearance. 'Please send up a few sandwiches and a bottle of sherry, and see that I am not disturbed. I have a lot of work to get through this afternoon.'

'Yes, sir.'

'Literary work.'

'Quite so, sir.'

'I am writing a film-drama — or perhaps I should say completing the final scenes of one,' said Dangelli. 'I find it an unusually arduous occupation. For the past three weeks I have scarcely written a line of my play. I have been waiting for an

inspiration. You know what an inspiration is?'

'I have seen it described in a dictionary, sir.'

'Quite so, Mapes. Well, that's the kind of thing I've been waiting for. I simply couldn't imagine how I was going to finish the last act of my play. But I've got my inspiration now.'

'I am very pleased to hear it, sir.'

'And can you guess where I got it?' the old professor went on.

With an expression of wooden immobility on his features, Mapes slowly shook his head. 'I really could not venture to offer a suggestion, sir. I have been informed that writers find their inspirations in so many queer places, sir.'

'Well, I found mine in an architect's office in the City. I met a dead man and had a long talk with him. That was queer, wasn't it?'

'It was indeed, sir.'

'And in the course of that talk, the dead man, without being in the least degree aware of the fact, gave me a priceless idea for the ending of my

film-drama. So if you will bring those sandwiches and close the door gently as you go out, I will now proceed to put that idea into words. Disconnect the telephone and remember that I am not at home to anybody.'

'Very good, sir.'

Left alone, Dangelli unlocked a small steel safe and took out an untidy bundle of manuscript and a formidable pile of blank sheets of paper. For the next two hours his pen moved with a facility that showed that his mind was no longer hampered by lack of definite ideas. With scarcely a pause his crabbed writing covered line after line. Page after page went to swell the pile of completed manuscript at his elbow.

It was evidence that the task he was engaged in was a labour of love. His bearded lips were set in a fixed grin as he wrote, and every now and then a low chuckle of amusement would escape them, as though he were conscious of a jest so piquant that it could not be enjoyed in silence.

He heard the distant purring of the

front door bell, and shortly afterwards the footsteps of the butler as he crossed the hall to answer the unknown caller. But still Dangelli's pen did not falter in its steady flow across the sheet of paper before him. He seemed totally unconscious of the growing murmur of voices outside the room. Only when the door was thrust unceremoniously open did he lay down his pen and raise his head — to meet the hostile gaze of Chief-Inspector Renshaw as he stood in the open doorway.

For a split-second a little flame seemed to glow and die in Dangelli's eyes as he noted that the police, officer's left hand held a blue paper, while his right was thrust deep in the pocket of his overcoat.

'Good afternoon, my dear Inspector. This is an unexpected pleasure.'

Totally ignoring the bland salutation, Renshaw turned and addressed the two plain-clothes detectives who hovered in the hall.

'One of you guard the door and the other the window,' he ordered crisply. 'Allow no one to pass in or out. I'll call if

I want your help inside.'

Turning round and still keeping his hands in their original positions, Inspector Renshaw closed the door with a backward thrust of his foot. Striding across the room, he stood looking down at the seated professor. The poise of Renshaw's stalwart figure was suggestive of alert determination; his expression that of a man who anticipates scoring the triumph of a lifetime.

'Compliments can wait,' he rapped out curtly. 'First I have a little business to transact.'

Professor Dangelli lifted his shoulders in a shrug of humorous resignation.

'Business? Coming from one of your profession, Inspector? That sounds somewhat ominous. However — '

He lowered his right hand below the level of the desk and slid open a drawer.

'Put your hands on the desk, and keep them there!' barked Renshaw, and at the same time his own right hand jerked out of his pocket, holding a heavy automatic trained on the seated figure. 'I'm not going to take any chances with the

Phantom of the Films!'

The old man sat back in his chair and a mocking smile flickered on his lips as he gazed at the unwavering circle of steel that menaced him. But he was careful to place his hands in the desired position.

'Really, Inspector, I had no idea that the methods of Scotland Yard were so highly dramatic! I would engage you for a part in my coming film were it not the fear that my offer might be misconstrued into a subtle attempt at bribery and corruption.'

'What were you about to take out of that drawer?' Renshaw demanded.

'Nothing, I assure you,' smiled the other. 'It is quite empty.'

'Then why did you open it?'

'To place something in it. The manuscript of the play I am writing.' Dangelli looked mildly amused. 'Can it be possible that you are about to take possession of it at the point of a loaded pistol? I assure you that it is scarcely worth it. As Shakespeare says, 'A poor thing but mine own' — '

'Stand away from that desk!'

Inspector Renshaw advanced warily until he was able to peer over the edge of the desk into the open drawer. It was empty.

'H'mph!' He pocketed his weapon with a grunt. 'So you were speaking the truth for once, Phantom!'

Dangelli's features expressed nothing more than a polite bewilderment.

'That is the second time you have addressed me by that ghostly appellation,' he said in a tone of mild protest. 'Do you intend those remarks for a cryptic kind of humour?'

'You'll soon see — when the time comes for us to laugh!'

Renshaw held up the blue document. 'Do you know what this is?'

'No. But I presume it is your official jest-book.'

Renshaw's face went red, but he swallowed the jibe.

'It's a warrant for your arrest,' he said impressively. 'But before I execute it I should like to have a little talk with you.'

'That is very wise of you, Inspector. A little talk beforehand may save a big

209

apology later on.'

'I'll chance the apology!' Renshaw burst out roughly. 'Mr. Phantom, I've got you where I want you!'

'Then won't you take a seat?' Dangelli said politely. 'And perhaps you'd like to remove your hat?'

Renshaw accepted the first invitation in silence; he affected not to hear the second. Seating himself at the desk, he produced a notebook and flattened it open with a triumphant smack of his hand.

'You think we've been fast asleep at the Yard,' he sneered. 'But we have not been asleep. There's enough evidence in this book to hang fifty Phantoms! Listen here — ' He twirled the pages rapidly. 'Exactly a month before Rattenbury was murdered you purchased a complete outfit for making films — '

'Hardly an indictable offence?' murmured the professor.

'About the same time your butler, James Mapes, underwent a course of instructions in the making of such films.'

'Mapes is a very adaptable person,'

Dangelli agreed calmly.

'And a few days before the murder you bought a cloak and slouch hat which has since been identified by the theatrical costumiers as those worn by the Phantom in the film that was shown at the Pantheon Theatre.'

Dangelli laughed softly.

'I think I have already mentioned the fact that I was writing a film-drama?' he asked suavely. 'If the facts which you have enumerated are proof of guilt, then you may as well string up every film producer in the country.'

'Wait! I haven't finished yet. We have further discovered that you are in the habit of making payments by cheque to a certain Andrea Mattioli, who purports to be the landlord of the premises in which Miss Dorene Grey's flat is situated.'

'Really? Then you might have gone further and discovered that Mattioli is employed by me to run 'The Laughing Mask' night club. Of course, I paid him,' the old man declaimed scornfully. 'Do you imagine that people are in the habit of working for nothing? Have you got any

more priceless clues in your little book? Pray read them if you have — I haven't enjoyed a hearty laugh for weeks!'

'Then laugh at this!'

Fumbling in his pocket, the detective slapped two photographs on the desk as he uttered the words. Glancing down, Dangelli saw that one was a snapshot of himself walking in a London street. The other was an enlargement of a section of celluloid ribbon and represented the Phantom of Films.

Renshaw smiled as he saw that he had at last penetrated the mask of studied indifference that the other had worn throughout the interview.

'It took a lot of patience to get you just in the position I wanted. I wasted several spools of films as I shadowed you about the streets, trying to snap you in the same attitude as that assumed by the Phantom. But in the end I succeeded. The negatives of these two photographs have been superimposed and printed into one composite positive. Except for the different dress, those two pictures have been pronounced by the experts to be

identical. I've known that you were the Phantom of the Films for weeks — and now I've proved it!'

Professor Dangelli rose from his seat and bowed with ceremonious gravity.

'Congratulations, my dear inspector,' he said.

'Then you don't deny that you are the Phantom?' cried the inspector, quick to take advantage of the implied admission.

'It would indeed be presumptuous of me to attempt to do so in the face of such overwhelming proof,' he said dryly.

'That's good enough for me.' Inspector Renshaw rose in his turn and laid his hand on the Professor's shoulder. 'I propose to take you into custody on suspicion of having caused the death of Amos Rattenbury. I warn you that — '

'And I warn you, Mr. Chief-Inspector Renshaw, of the C.I.D.!' With a quick, sinuous movement the old man shook off the detaining grasp and came a step nearer to his captor, his frail form trembling with rage, his eyes glowing like live coals. 'I warn you that if you arrest me it will be the last arrest you will make

in your official career!'

'Threats, hey?'

'No — just warnings — and I hope for your sake that they will prove words to the wise. As I am a living man I swear that my arrest will mean the coat being stripped from your back before you are a fortnight older! Don't stand there scowling at me like that. Can't you realize that I'm doing you a kindness by telling you this instead of letting you make a fool of yourself in open court? Your so-called evidence against me is worthless. No magistrate would commit me for trial on it.'

'You seem mighty sure of yourself,' growled Renshaw, drawing back slightly. As he stood there, wary but undecided, he looked like a great mastiff momentarily daunted by the threats of a spitting cat.

Professor Dangelli thrust his hand into his pocket and tossed a notebook on the desk.

'You've shown me what you've got in your little book; now have a look what's in mine. On the first page you will see a list of names of eminent clergymen,

headed by the Bishop of Westerham. At the time that Rattenbury was being murdered they were attending a conference at the Diocesan Hall in that City. I was present too, and if you get busy with that telephone you will find that every one of those reverend gentlemen is prepared to back my alibi.'

The police officer stared at the list of names like a man in a dream. If the professor was bluffing, it was the most gigantic and daring bluff that he had ever heard of.

'That seems to rule you out, Professor, if what you say is true,' he admitted after a long pause.

Dangelli jerked his head towards the desk.

'The telephone is at your disposal if you have any doubt about the matter,' he said icily.

Renshaw declined the invitation with a sullen shake of his head. 'I guess I can check up later. I'm in no hurry. I can wait for my man — whether he's you or somebody else.'

'Excellent!' he cried gaily. 'Everything

comes to him who waits, you know. But you will not have to wait very long, my dear inspector. My film-drama will be ready for production in a few days.'

'Your film-drama!' With difficulty Renshaw managed to control his voice as he uttered the words. 'What in the name of madness has your fool film to do with us?'

Professor Dangelli beamed as he accompanied his uninvited guest to the door.

'When Clifford Baxter produces my film, I will produce the man who murdered Amos Rattenbury!'

'Is that a promise, sir?' cried the detective.

Dangelli's smile broadened into a sardonic grin.

'Does it sound like a threat, my dear inspector?' he asked blandly. 'Good afternoon, sir. I trust to have the pleasure of welcoming you and a hefty contingent of your merry men at the studio on the great day.'

'I'll be there,' said Renshaw, smiling grimly, 'with a nice pair of reception handcuffs!'

Professor Dangelli laughed more loudly than the somewhat feeble jest seemed to deserve.

'I'll try my best to find a suitable wearer for them,' was his parting shot. 'You shall not be baulked of your prey a second time, if I can possibly help it!'

19

Professor Dangelli had declared that the Press would give him all the publicity he required for his coming film, and subsequent events proved that he was right. The most astute and energetic press agent could not have aroused public interest to a greater pitch of excitement than did the verdicts of the two coroners' juries who inquired into the deaths of the victims. 'Wilful murder against some person or person unknown,' was the finding in each instance, and though the newspapers carefully refrained from identifying the Phantom of the Films with the perpetrator of the crimes, it did not take long for the intelligent readers of their pages to fill in the blank for themselves.

The police and public alike were agreed in the conviction that once the Phantom was arrested there would be no need to look further for the double murderer.

Who was the Phantom? Who was the

cunning, cold-blooded killer who hid behind that gruesome *nom de guerre*? What detective could arrest, what jury could convict, what executioner could hang an intangible being whose only evidence of reality were a shrouded flickering figure projected on a screen, and a ghostly, bodiless voice?

He might be anybody. He might be anywhere.

While interest was still at fever heat, subtle hints began to appear in the Press to the effect that a certain Italian scientist was on the point of producing a film which he confidently declared would expose, not only the identity of the Phantom, but also the method by which he was enabled to commit his seemingly impossible crimes.

Energetic and persistent young men, each with a notebook and an insatiable thirst for information, began to haunt the vicinity of the Baxter Film Studios. Clifford Baxter himself, badgered, besieged and bombarded with endless volleys of questions, began to wear a harassed look on his rugged face. It was useless for him

to tell the reporters that he knew nothing whatever of the proposed ending on the film which he was producing. Finally, he called his tormentors together and addressed them in a body:

'Look here, you chaps,' he said. 'I'm not averse to seeing my name in print — in the right columns, of course — and I don't object to my show getting its share of any of the ballyhoo that's going to be spread around. I'll allow that we're at present engaged on a film that's going to be called *The Phantom Stabber*, and I won't deny that it's got something to do with the Phantom of the Films that everyone is talking about. But when you ask me what the plot of the piece is, well, I guess you've asked me one too many. The author doles out the script of the various parts, one scene at a time, and not a soul except himself knows what's coming next. Believe me, boys, my leading man doesn't know yet whether he's playing the hero, the villain, or the low comedian. That's not the truth, anyway, but it'll raise a laugh. The rest of it *is* the truth, the whole truth, and

nothing but the truth. There's only one man who knows how the play's going to end — Professor Niccolo Dangelli. And he is determined to keep it under his hat! So you boys had better leave me alone, and quit haunting this place. Go home and think out a few thousand nice new adjectives and superlatives and things, and get ready to churn out some red-hot copy when our first big first-night show comes off.'

There was a chorus of disappointed protest from the crowd of reporters.

'Clifford, you're an oyster,' declared one, but Baxter gave a twisted grin as he shook his head.

'You're wrong, laddie. At the present moment I represent a chicken sitting on a strange egg, not knowing whether it's going to hatch out a chick, or a duckling, or a lively little snake. That's me, boys — just waiting, and looking pleasant and hoping for the best; and if you're wise boys, that's what you'll do.'

He began to shepherd the group towards the door. 'And now I'm going to be that busy that I'd like to see a view of

your backs better'n anything on earth. Keep going as you are down that passage, and you'll find the door marked 'Way Out' right in front of you.'

It is no exaggeration to state that the general excitement of the hunt for the elusive Phantom had spread to the members of the cast of *The Phantom Stabber*, otherwise they would never have consented to the conditions imposed on them by their eccentric employer. Artists of established reputation are not accustomed to have their parts handed to them 'in penny numbers' — to quote the trenchant words of one indignant actor. Terry Hilton flattered himself that he was what is professionally termed a 'quick study', but even he was occasionally hard put to it to memorize vital lines at a few hours' notice. It says much for the persuasive powers of the smooth-voiced professor that he had contrived to keep his company together until they had reached the final scene that was due to be 'shot' that day.

With an audacity that was almost fantastic, Dangelli had applied to the

Commissioner of Police for permission to engage a number of uniformed police officers to assist in the last scene of the film. To the astonishment of everybody except himself, that permission had been promptly granted, and on a scale which erred only on the side of liberality. He got six constables, a sergeant, and a full-blown Chief-Inspector.

The old professor rubbed his hands in delight as he saw the imposing array of blue-coated stalwarts waiting like a guard of honour for his arrival in the studio, and his pleasure did not appear to diminish as he recognized the familiar features of Inspector Renshaw under the peaked cap of the officer in command.

'All present and correct, sir,' the inspector reported with a smart salute. 'I didn't forget your words the other day, so I asked permission to fall in with the 'movie-squad'. I thought you might be able to find me a place in the picture.'

'Delighted to see you, my dear Inspector,' the old man returned dryly. 'I dare say you'll have plenty to do before the day is out. Our little gathering seems

to have every indication of being quite an interesting reunion of old friends. Sir Digby Hilton, your Assistant Commissioner, has promised to honour me with his distinguished presence. Mr. Julian Rotheimer, the manager of the Pantheon, has sacrificed his moustache in order to play the part of his murdered brother, and Miss Dorene Grey is to appear as her own charming self.'

'Yes,' agreed the inspector slowly. 'It only needs the Phantom to make the circle complete.'

A smile, cold and satiny, flitted over Dangelli's face.

'Oh, he'll show up, never fear, when he gets his entrance-cue.'

'Is that so?' Inspector Renshaw's usually phlegmatic voice was jerky with an undercurrent of excitement. 'Then I reckon that his entrance will be *my* cue to do a little quick business that's not down in your book of words!'

During the short silence that followed, the eyes of the two men met, wary and challenging, like the blades of two fencers, each uncertain of the other's

skill. Then the Italian broke the tension by lifting his shoulders indifferently and motioning towards the door.

'Would you care to have a look at the set which I have had specially constructed for the occasion?' he asked politely. 'I should value your opinion whether it is a good imitation of the real thing.'

The wide and lofty hall of the studio proper was a scene of orderly last-minute bustle. Here, under a roof that soared aloft like the dome of a cathedral, was a complete life-size model of the office block in New Cambridge Street, together with the frontage of the buildings in the slightly narrower turning, which ran by one side. With a lavish disregard of expense seldom seen in a studio on this side of the Atlantic, Dangelli had insisted on scrupulous accuracy down to the smallest detail that was likely to come before the eye of the camera. Though the framework of the four stories was but roughly squared timber, and the seemingly solid walls mere lath and plaster; though its flimsiness of construction was such as might have caused a violent

brainstorm in the mind of any Borough Surveyor called upon to pass it as fulfilling the requirements of public safety, the general effect was as if a section of the West-Central District had been transported bodily and dumped intact in that suburban studio.

'It's the real thing all right,' said Renshaw with an approving nod. 'But couldn't you have used the actual buildings?'

Dangelli grinned as he shook his head.

'But what would you police have said if we started erecting camera-stage on the sidewalk of New Cambridge Street and blocked the traffic with sound-damping screens and a battery of sun-arcs? To say nothing of the crowds that would gather to watch our proceedings. Believe me, it comes cheaper in the long run to fake a set unless we can exclude the public altogether. Mr. Boyd-Pennington planned this one, and I think you will admit he has done his work well.'

Inspector Renshaw glanced round quickly.

'Boyd-Pennington?' he repeated. 'That

name sounds familiar, but I can't exactly place its owner.'

'He was the man your mobile patrol pulled in on the night when the cancelled contract was found in Rattenbury's safe. He was taken to Scotland Yard, where he explained that he had just left his office — that building over there — ' Dangelli jabbed an explanatory finger in the direction of the scenic frontage which, situated in the street by the side of the larger building, represented the architect's office. 'You accepted his explanation — or rather the Assistant Commissioner did — and he was released with suitable apologies.'

'And is this man taking part in the film?' asked the other curiously.

Dangelli shook his head.

'The main part of his duties ended when the set was built, but he is still busy superintending the correct arrangement of the furniture in the room which represents Rattenbury's office. Care to have a look at it?'

Renshaw accepted the invitation with alacrity, and the two men passed through

the swing doors and along the artistically dingy corridor.

They passed through the bare little waiting room, with Mifflin's untidy desk set angle-wise near the door. The next instant the inspector was staring open-mouthed at the same scene that had met his gaze when he had entered Amos Rattenbury's office of the afternoon of the murder.

'I should never have believed it possible!' he cried. 'Every detail is perfect and accurate — even the pictures on the walls and that stinking incense stuff in the burner on the desk. It only wants a corpse to complete the picture.'

A smirk of gratification was on the professor's face as he listened to this unstudied praise.

'It ought to be something like the original, seeing that I bought the whole contents of Rattenbury's suite almost immediately after the inquest. But, of course, even the original furniture would have been useless for my purpose unless placed in its original position. I have to thank Mr. Boyd-Pennington here for the

careful manner in which he drew out the plan that enabled this to be accomplished. Mr. Boyd-Pennington,' he added, addressing the little round-faced man who was putting the finishing touches to the reconstructed room, 'this is the gentleman who is playing the part of the police-inspector in my film.'

The architect responded with a friendly nod.

'Pleased to meet you, sir.' He turned to Dangelli. 'I think that finishes my part of the business. But I'll remain around, if you have no objection, in case I can be of assistance in any little detail that has been overlooked.'

'Do so, by all means,' responded the professor, 'and allow me to congratulate you on a very fine and accurate piece of work. If Amos Rattenbury could return from the grave he would think himself back in his old office, eh? But this is not likely to happen, and perhaps it's as well that it isn't. If every victim of a crime were to revisit the earth and denounce his murderer, Scotland Yard would soon find its occupation gone!'

Mr. Cyril Boyd-Pennington smiled a superior smile.

'I fear I am a hopeless sceptic in matters supernatural,' he declared. 'In my opinion there is no greater falsehood than the old saying, 'Murder will out.' A man once dead is dead for all time, whether he dies in his bed or in his boots. Rattenbury will lie in his grave until — '

The confident voice faltered and tailed off strangely into silence. Glancing at the speaker, the two men saw that his ruddy face had suddenly become devoid of its healthy colour; his staring eyes were fixed on the door with an expression of frozen horror.

Standing in the doorway was the living image of the murdered man!

For a fractional moment the four figures remained motionless in a tense, dramatic silence. It was the Professor who spoke first:

'I don't think I mentioned to you that Mr. Rotheimer was playing the part of his brother?' he remarked carelessly. 'The resemblance is really very striking, is it not? If one did not possess your

scepticism in occult matters Mr. Boyd-Pennington, one might almost be tempted to imagine that at least one unavenged victim had returned to even up the scales of Justice.'

Gradually Boyd-Pennington's features lost their rigid, tight-drawn expression and resumed their usual cherubic smoothness. Either he was unaware of the mocking note hidden in the professor's silk-smooth tones, or he chose purposely to ignore it.

'For the moment I thought I had seen a ghost,' he confessed with a laugh that was slightly overdone. 'The atmosphere of your creepy murder-film is beginning to get the better of my poor nerves. I'll go in the grounds and have a quiet smoke.'

'If you leave this studio you'll remain outside until the film is shot,' snapped the professor. 'We're working behind locked doors today. There are too many press-hounds sniffing about outside before the right moment. So you'll have to decide right now whether you're going to go or stay. Which is it to be?'

Boyd-Pennington hesitated, his plump

white hand fondling his shaven lip.

'I think I'll — '

The strident clang of a bell cut short his sentence.

'Too late!' cried Dangelli, and for an instant the white gleam of teeth showed between his grey beard. 'The show is about to begin, and you'll have to see it through whether you like it or not.'

Hard upon his words came the sound of Baxter's stentorian voice bellowing through his megaphone.

'Silence, please, and clear the stage! Beginners take their places for the last scene of *The Phantom Stabber*.'

20

Deep, unbroken silence reigned within the great studio — a silence almost uncanny because there were so many people present.

Like a regiment of drifting shadows the operating staff went about their accustomed tasks, their footsteps deadened by the felt-soled shoes which each man wore, their hands mutely fulfilling the function of tongues by gestures and the occasional exhibition of a printed card. One half of the studio showed starkly white under the powerful reflectors of the electric arcs, the other half was plunged in a shadowy gloom all the deeper by contrast. And amid the gloom dim figures moved, tending with practised touch the silently running cameras and the other apparatus.

It must be admitted that Professor Dangelli had made no attempt to invest his drama with literary graces and embellishments. The language that he had

put into the mouths of his characters was just plain, everyday prose, without polish and with very little art in its arrangement. Yet there was not a person present, not even those taking part in the play, who did not feel an ever-increasing thrill of excitement as the plain, unvarnished history of the crime began to unfold itself before them.

Dangelli, once he had handed over the reins to Clifford Baxter, had wisely left the producer to himself by slipping away unobtrusively, and Inspector Renshaw, who had cogent reasons of his own for keeping a watchful eye on him, found himself searching the shadows in vain for a glimpse of the tall, slender figure of the Italian professor. But the man who claimed to hold the secret of the Phantom of the Films had eliminated himself completely.

In the course of his wanderings about the darkened part of the studio he found himself by the side of Sir Digby Hilton, and the mutely questioning glance that the Assistant Commissioner gave convinced him that he, too, had noticed the

professor's absence.

'Where is he?' Sir Digby whispered, his lips close to the inspector's ear, and there was no need for him to elaborate the significant pronoun.

Renshaw shrugged and shook his head.

'But he can't go far, sir,' he answered in the same low tone. 'I have one of my men at every door of the studio. Excuse me asking, sir, but are you armed?'

Sir Digby nodded and patted his hip, and the inspector, apparently satisfied, glided away.

It was a queer train of thought that filtered through the mind of the Assistant Commissioner as he stood there in the darkness. He was a man of the world, shrewd, far-seeing, with a mind that was eminently practical. Not for an instant did he believe that the eccentric professor would make good his boast. The idea of an outsider solving a mystery that had defied the resources of Scotland Yard was too absurd for a man to entertain. But the man might possess inside information regarding the crime, and this might be his crazy mode of making that information

known to the police. Inside information! In those two words lay the explanation why Sir Digby had consented to take this farce seriously. The professor might be vain, pretentious, egotistic to the verge of megalomania, but somewhere in the recesses of his warped brain there might lurk the one clue needful to put the police on the right track in their hunt for the killer.

What if Dangelli was himself the Phantom? If the man's brain really was unbalanced, such a masquerade would be a natural sequence. The man's theatricality, his passion for the films, his impish delight in showing his superiority to the official police force — everything fitted in. Yet in the face of this theory was the undeniable fact that on the afternoon of Rattenbury's murder Dangelli had been fifty miles away. His alibi had been confirmed by the unimpeachable testimony of a score of clergymen, including a bishop.

As an alibi it was perfect — almost too perfect, Digby decided cynically. Never before had Dangelli attended such a

conference of divines nor had he shown the least interest in such matters until that particular day, and his presence at Westerham at such an irreproachable gathering seemed almost to indicate that he had had foreknowledge that the crime was about to be committed. Most decidedly Dangelli was a man well worth watching, and Sir Digby felt more pleased than ever that he had accepted the invitation to be present at the filming of he final scene. It would be hard indeed if his day proved to be entirely wasted.

But where was Dangelli now? Why had he chosen the moment of the approaching climax to efface himself so completely? With an effort of will, Sir Digby banished his futile speculations and applied himself to a study of what was going on around him.

Apparently the drama was rapidly approaching the point when the victim would meet his appointed fate. Julian Rotheimer, looking the very image of his dead brother, was seated in his office. Dorene Grey had just been announced by an actor who was but a thinly disguised

replica of Albert Mifflin.

'All right, I'm expecting her,' said 'Rattenbury', glancing in the mirror to settle his tie and smooth his sleek hair. 'Show her in, and see that we are not disturbed.'

'I understand, sir,' smirked 'Mifflin' as he disappeared.

Almost immediately Dorene made her entrance. She wore the hat and fur-trimmed long coat, over the choosing of which Dangelli had expended such care. Her beautiful face was made-up to find favour in the eye of the camera, which, expressing its recorded image only through the medium of black and white, requires a different set of values to those which find favour through human eyes.

'Good afternoon, Miss Grey,' said the theatrical agent. 'You're a trifle early for your appointment, Miss.'

The girl glanced at the clock on the mantelpiece.

'I thought you said five o'clock, Mr. Rattenbury,' she said in surprise, 'and it is just on the hour now.'

'A few minutes one way or the other is

not of much importance. Now that you're here we may as well get to business. I've had the contract drafted out, and it's only necessary for you to attach your signature.' He placed a folded paper on the desk before her. 'You already know the terms of the contract.'

The girl nodded.

'Then be good enough to sign.'

Dorene complied. The agent glanced at the signature, blotted it carefully, and placed the contract in the safe.

'Can't we forget business for an hour or two?' he then asked slowly. 'How does a little supper party tonight appeal to you — just you and I?'

'I'm afraid it does not appeal to me at all,' said the girl in a tone of quiet decision.

'No? Well, it's a pity.' The agent drew out a corpulent cigar and lit it. 'Intended to give the leading part in my show to a girl not half so beautiful — and not a quarter as talented — as you. You might be able to persuade me to exchange your roles.'

Dorene shook her head. 'I'm a very

poor hand at persuading people.'

The man's flabby features creased in an evil grin.

'But I am very easily persuaded — after supper.'

Dorene rose abruptly to her feet, crossed to the door and grasped the handle.

'Why, it's locked!' she cried.

'Not locked,' he explained easily. 'It fastens with a spring.'

Turning, she confronted him with flashing eyes.

'Open that door at once, Mr. Rattenbury!'

'All in good time, my dear. Surely you would not cut short the pleasure of my little interview? I don't think I've ever met a girl so exquisite — so adorable — '

She struggled as his arms tightened about her shoulders. A split second later the man was recoiling as he caught the silvery glint of rounded metal in her gloved hand.

'No, it's not a revolver,' she said, reading the thought which had turned his face into a mask of terror. 'It's something

better — a police whistle, given me by someone who understood your character better than I did. If you do not open that door at once I'll rouse the neighbourhood.'

'And get your pretty name in all the newspapers,' sneered the man. 'Have you thought of that?'

Dorene's eyes, searching frantically for some means of escape, had seen the open window and the iron trellis of the fire ladder. The man stopped speaking and changed his tone as he saw her intention. But she was already at the window.

'Come back, you little fool!' he cried. 'Can't you see I was only testing your capacity for expressing facial emotions? Come back, and we'll stick to strict business. Come back!' He raised his voice to a shout as she began to run lightly down the iron steps. 'Now's your chance — you'll make a certain hit!'

Thus far the play had proceeded smoothly, but now at the very moment when the sensational climax should have been forthcoming, the scene appeared to come to an abrupt and tantalizing end.

The machinery of the cameras ceased to revolve, the dazzling arcs were switched off, all except one which still continued to shed its narrow beam on the interior of the silent and deserted office.

Sir Digby Hilton began to shift uneasily as the first feeling of disappointment caused by this tame anti-climax slowly resolved itself into a feeling of anger. It gradually began to dawn on his mind that he had been badly fooled.

'Well?' he cried irritably, turning to Clifford Baxter. 'What are you waiting for? Is that the end of the wonderful drama that we've heard so much about?'

'*Not quite, Sir Digby,*' said a high-pitched, strident voice. '*The farce is over — but the tragedy is only just about to begin!*'

Into the circle of the spotlight there stepped a weird and terrifying figure. Cloaked from shoulder to heel, masked from brow to chin, with even the contours of his head hidden beneath the drooping brim of his wide felt hat, it was an image at once inscrutable yet familiar. A hushed cry of recognition from all

present greeted its appearance.

'The Phantom of the Films!'

The masked figure raised its hand and bowed with the gesture of a monarch acknowledging the plaudits of his subjects.

'It is indeed the Phantom, good friends and enemies,' said the cracked voice from behind the black mask. 'You are privileged to behold him in the flesh, and not in the film. It may, however, prove a dearly bought privilege to some of those present.'

Sir Digby and Inspector Renshaw stepped a pace forward, moving as one man. In the right hand of each was a heavy revolver, trained on the man who stood like a black shadow in the spotlight's glare.

'The game's up, Phantom!' snapped Renshaw. 'Every door is guarded and every guard is armed.'

The cloaked shoulders rose in a polite shrug.

'Indeed? Then you have the advantage of me there.'

He spread his gloved hands as he

spoke, demonstrating their emptiness.

'Besides,' Sir Digby added in a quieter tone than that used by his subordinate. 'We know who you are. Resistance is useless.'

With a sudden movement the Phantom tore the mask from his face and hurled it to the ground.

'Dangelli!' cried Renshaw as he saw the well-known bearded features. 'I knew it all along!'

'Your certitude is somewhat late, brother,' smiled the professor, 'but there is no denying its accuracy. The bogey Phantom has done its work — or nearly so; by all means let his hideous trappings reveal the much less terrifying man beneath. I suppose it is needless for me to admit further that I really am Professor Niccolo Dangelli.'

Dangelli bowed gravely.

'Your advice is good. Rest assured, never before will you have arrested so quiet and so willing a prisoner — that is,' he added swiftly, 'if you can arrest me!'

'We can arrest you all right,' Renshaw ground out between set teeth.

'Ah, don't be too sure of that.' A ring of menace seemed to creep into the smooth accents. 'Do you think that I should have thrust my head into the lion's mouth if I were in any danger of being hauled to a prison cell — and thence to the scaffold? Do you imagine that I am fool enough to come within reach of your clutches unless I was sure that I could slip through your fingers in the twinkling of an eye? You have a long reach, a sure reach, you gentlemen of the official police, but the slippery Phantom now, as ever, is beyond it!'

'How?' came the harsh demand.

'Because he can escape you any moment he chooses,' was the smooth reply.

Sir Digby started at the speaker in stupefied amazement. Was the man mad? Did he contemplate suicide? There he stood, calm, smiling, unruffled. He was a prisoner, alone, surrounded, without hope of succour. Before him was the condemned cell; the beam with the ghastly dangling noose. He stood in the very shadow of the scaffold — yet he

could smile and talk of escape!

'Enough of this nonsense!' Renshaw broke in roughly. 'Put up — '

'Wait!' Dangelli hissed sharply.

'Yes — wait,' echoed Digby, and the inspector fell back like a sullen hound whipped off an exhausted fox that had been run to earth after a long and wearisome chase.

'I thank you, Sir Digby.' The professor made a polite inclination of his head. 'In return for your courtesy I will make my explanation as brief as possible — '

'Yes, do!' With a sardonic chuckle Inspector Renshaw produced a pair of handcuffs and jingled them suggestively. 'How is the slippery Phantom going to wriggle out of these?'

'By merely reminding you' — the silky voice was now addressed directly at the inspector — 'that in your blindness you assumed, without one particle of real evidence to support your conclusion — that the Phantom committed the two murders. Take your mind back, my dear Inspector and think, please, think a little! Granted that I am the Phantom, how

could I have murdered Rattenbury when 1 was fifty miles away at the time? How could I murder Mrs. Peters when I was with this young lady,' he stepped forward and drew the wondering Dorene to his side, 'ordering the very charming clothes which she now wears? Ponder well on those knotty points, my dear Inspector, and then you may begin to understand how I am going to slip through your hands. I do not fear the law for the simple reason that I have transgressed no law. The dreaded Phantom which has hung like a nightmare over London, making the police work overtime and providing the gentlemen of the Press with a thousand grisly titbits with which to tickle their readers' palates, was but a mild, innocuous, milk-and-water apparition after all! His gravest misdemeanour consisted of confessing that he had killed a man when in fact, he hadn't done anything of the kind.'

Very slowly, almost as though his actions were part of a ritual, Inspector Renshaw slipped his revolver into one pocket and the handcuffs into another.

'Better keep the snaps handy, Inspector,' advised Dangelli. 'You may have your prisoner after all.'

'Then you know who is the real murderer?' gasped Digby.

'Assuredly. Did I not promise that everything would be made clear at the filming of my drama? I should be but a poor playwright if I sent my audience away no wiser than when they came.' He sank his voice to a whisper as he went on rapidly. 'Allow me five minutes' private conversation in here with this young lady, and I may be able to give you the proof you need.'

'Is a private interview really necessary?' demurred the Assistant Commissioner, with a questioning glance in the direction of Dorene.

'Absolutely necessary.'

'Then I have no objection, providing, of course, that Miss Grey is willing — '

'To trust her life in my hands?' Dangelli completed the hesitating sentence. 'What do you say, Dorene?'

'Of course,' came the girl's answer without the slightest hesitation. 'Professor

Dangelli is my best friend.'

At a nod from the Assistant Commissioner the rest of the men withdrew, leaving the girl alone in the presence of the unmasked Phantom. Scarcely had the door closed behind when a shrill scream of terror vibrated through the studio.

'Help! I am stabbed!' came a gasping cry in Dorene's voice.

Renshaw spun round like a top.

'He's fooled us, Chief!' he cried in bitter triumph. 'The Phantom wanted his third victim — and he's got her under our very noses!'

In a body they dashed back into the room. Terry Hilton uttered a cry of horrified despair at the sight that met his eyes.

21

In the centre of the room the Phantom stood like a sinister, sable-cloaked statue. On the floor, in exactly the same spot where Rattenbury's corpse had been found, lay Dorene Grey, her hand pressed tightly to her breast immediately above her heart.

'Madman!' Terry cried fiercely. 'What have you done?'

Not a muscle of the Phantom's body stirred as he stood looking fixedly at the inanimate form at his feet. Only his lips moved.

'On the contrary, gentlemen, I have been the means of saving her from death for the second time,' he said calmly. 'But for the coat of finely tempered steel chainmail, which I ordered the tailor to insert between the cloth and the silk lining of the coat she is wearing, that dagger would have reached her heart.'

'Dagger?' jerked out Renshaw. 'What dagger?'

Dangelli stooped quickly, pulled aside the fold of the long grey coat, and picked up a short, keen-bladed knife. With growing surprise, the two police officers saw that the point had been snapped off short.

'The shirt of mail, which Miss Grey was all unconsciously wearing, came from my collection of ancient arms and armour,' the professor resumed his explanation. 'It was made to the order of the infamous Lucrezia Borgia, and the old Italian armourers did their work well. When presently I rip that ancient relic from the very up-to-date coat in which it is concealed, you will see that the finely-woven steel links, though light and pliable, are quite capable of protecting its wearer from anything less penetrative than a bullet. When the dagger came into contact with the mail, its blade snapped short, as you can see.'

'But why did you strike such a blow?' demanded Sir Digby.

Professor Dangelli shook his head.

'That deadly stroke was not aimed by my hand.'

'Whose then?'

'Come with me, and you shall see both the man, and the manner by which his fiendish work was accomplished.'

Turning on his heel, Dangelli led the way out of the room. Terry stayed behind, comforting the still-shocked girl. Dangelli led the others down the stairs, across the side street and up into the room which represented the office in Little Cambridge Street that was in the occupation of Mr. Cyril Boyd-Pennington.

A strange and unexpected tableau met their gaze as the professor pushed open the door and signed to them to enter.

James Mapes, the butler, and Vincenzio, the chauffeur, were holding Boyd-Pennington firmly by the arms.

'This is your man,' said Dangelli, pointing to the architect.

A cry of fierce denial broke from the prisoner's ashy lips. 'It's a lie! I did not kill Miss Grey — I swear I have not quitted this room for the past hour!'

'Save your oaths for the witness-box

— if you dare to enter it at your trial,' Dangelli interrupted coldly. 'You had no need to enter Rattenbury's office when he was murdered; no footprints showed on the soft soil of the garden in which Mrs. Peters' body was found — yet in every case yours was the hand that launched the fatal blow. But you struck from a distance. Your victim in every instance was shot, not stabbed, and by using as a projectile a weapon usually wielded by hand, you succeeded — I should say almost succeeded — in investing your crimes with a mystery which approached the supernatural.'

The Assistant Commissioner was regarding the speaker with a puzzled frown.

'How could these people have been shot?' he asked. 'In not a single instance was the report of a firearm heard.'

'I do not recollect mentioning the word 'firearm',' the professor returned dryly. 'Our ingenious friend used one of the smaller types of pneumatic bomb-throwers which were substituted for the usual trench-mortars on the Italian

front at the time when Captain Boyd-Pennington's battery was serving with the Second Army. These guns operated on the same principle as an airgun. They were introduced in the nature of an experiment; only a few were used, and those few were soon withdrawn. But the artillery captain was quick to see their usefulness for other purposes besides warfare. Powerful, silent, accurate, with an effective range of over three hundred yards — here was a novel weapon ready to his hand with which he could slay with impunity.'

'But where is such a weapon?' demanded Digby, glancing about the room.

'Here!' said Dangelli.

There were numerous instruments used in surveying scattered about the room, and as the professor spoke he laid his hand on a tripod that supported a brass tube that looked for all the world like a short, squat telescope.

'That?' The Assistant Commissioner exploded in a fit of laughter. 'What mare's nest have you found now, Professor? That

instrument is nothing more than a theodolite, which every land surveyor uses for measuring angles!'

'It certainly has all the outward appearance of such an instrument,' admitted the unruffled professor, 'and therein lies the ingenuity of the contrivance. So innocent does it appear, that its owner could — and actually did — carry it openly in the street without anyone suspecting that he was in possession of an engine of destruction. Unless examined by an expert, it would pass as a theodolite. All its fittings, the minutely graduated scales which measure its arc of elevation, the delicate vernier which measures its angle of direction, all are identical with those of a real theodolite — and needless to say, they would enable the tube to be sighted with deadly accuracy. So much for the outward appearance of the engine. Now tell me if you have ever seen a theodolite capable of being manipulated thus — ?'

Dangelli fumbled among the mechanism for several seconds before his fingers found and grasped a small brass lever.

This he worked up and down about a dozen times, and it was evident that each successive stroke required a greater force.

'It grows stiffer as the pressure of the air increases,' he explained. 'The principle is similar to the American Sims-Dudley pneumatic cannon, formerly used by the U.S. Artillery for projecting shells containing nitro-gelatin and other explosives too sensitive to be fired by the usual propelling charge. But of course that was a much more powerful weapon, working under a pressure of 11,000lbs., and having a range of 3,000 yards. But this handier weapon was quite good enough for Boyd-Pennington's purpose. It is now charged with compressed air ready to fire. It is only necessary to give a slight turn of this innocent-looking milled screw, and — '

There was a soft thud and the tube gave a vicious backward jerk on its heavy tripod stand. Then Cyril Boyd-Pennington spoke.

'You win, Professor. I'll hand it to you right now, and cheat you of the pleasure of hearing your own voice explaining how

clever you were in finding out the why and wherefore.' Into the architect's ruddy features had crept a marble-like pallor; his dull eyes held the look of a man who sees no hope. 'Yes, it's true, I killed — '

He sagged forward with a convulsive shudder, and the next moment his captors were supporting the weight of a lifeless man.

A few moments later Professor Dangelli drew the Assistant Commissioner aside.

'I thought that he might take the short way out of his trouble, but nobody on earth could have prevented him,' he said in a low voice. 'He must have had the capsule of cyanide in his mouth all the time, and he crushed it between his teeth the moment he realized the game was up.'

'He might have waited a bit,' Sir Digby returned in an aggrieved tone. 'His abrupt departure left unexplained a whole lot of things that I should like to know.'

'I can explain everything in a few words, including the sinister masquerade on my part which must seem inexplicable

to you. As an old friend of Dorene Grey's family, I knew her uncle, Cyril Boyd-Pennington, quite well by sight. He was vicious and unprincipled even in those days before the war. He borrowed heavily, from Dorene's father among others, and when he was reported 'Missing, believed dead', he did not trouble to contradict the report, so far as his creditors were concerned. They believed that he had met a hero's death while serving in Italy.

'I knew better, however,' he resumed presently. 'I happened to come across him again after the war, and when Dr. Grey died, leaving Boyd-Pennington next in succession to Dorene to the fortune which I well knew would accrue from the old doctor's invention, I made it my business to keep a watchful eye on the doings of Cyril Boyd-Pennington. I fancy I have mentioned before that I make a hobby of detective work?' The old professor smiled faintly. 'Well, I almost rode my hobby to death gathering data regarding the uncle of the girl in which I took such an interest — a fatherly interest, needless to say. I found out very

little to his credit. He was leading a very festive life, gambling heavily, and was up to his ears in debt.

'Then there happened a curious incident which at first sight seemed to have no connection whatever with the man I was keeping under observation. But I was on the lookout for curious incidents, and I devoted more attention to it than did the police or the coroner's jury. A man, a homeless tramp, was found on the open heath at Blackheath, stabbed to the heart, and lying within fifty yards of the window of Boyd-Pennington's house. It seemed a strange, motiveless crime, for the victim had spent the previous night in a Deptford casual ward, and was known to be practically penniless. But it aroused very little interest at the time and that little quickly subsided when a verdict of suicide was returned at the inquest.'

Dangelli paused and indulged in a dry chuckle.

'Yes, everybody was satisfied,' he went on, 'except a certain queer old professor who was generally regarded as having a great many bees in his bonnet. He

conceived the ridiculous idea that the tramp had been slain by a method hitherto unemployed in the annals of crime. He even went so far as to break the law by paying a burglarious visit to Boyd-Pennington's house one night, and what he found there was sufficient to root the absurd idea in the old professor's mind more firmly than ever. Sir Digby, that old professor was myself, and the thing that he discovered in Boyd-Pennington's house at Blackheath stands there!'

And Dangelli pointed to the theodolite-gun.

'After that,' Dangelli continued, 'I set myself the problem why the ex-captain of artillery should have gone to the trouble of disguising a pneumatic bomb-thrower as an ordinary theodolite instrument. Surely not simply in order to slay a homeless outcast? I spent a whole month tracing the past history and the recent movements of that tramp, and in the end I was surer than ever that he had not the remotest connection with the man who had murdered him. He was just a piece of

human flotsam who had chanced to drift across the heath during his wanderings from one casual ward to another. Yet Boyd-Pennington had expended a considerable sum of money and had even risked his neck to kill him. Why? Like a spark of light the answer seemed to flash through my mind with a clarity that made me marvel how I could have remained for so long puzzling in the dark. The killing of the tramp was but a tentative experiment with his novel weapon. He was merely testing its capabilities before aiming it at higher game!

'There was no need for me to seek far to guess in what direction the ultimate target would lie. A single life stood between him and a fortune of two million pounds. A man who had taken one life, simply in order to test his gun, would not be likely to hesitate to fire a second shot to win such a prize. Dorene Grey, the girl whom I had promised her father to protect, was in deadly peril. I alone could save her. Unaided by the police, I must pit my wits against the cunning of this monster in human form. It would be a

struggle of brain versus brain, with a clear arena and no favour, and, frankly, the prospect was not wholly unpleasing to me. I think I have already explained that I have a penchant for detective work?'

'You have told me so on more occasions than one, my dear professor,' Digby said dryly. 'But pray continue.'

'In the course of my inquiries I had renewed my acquaintance with one of my fellow countrymen who had fallen on evil days — in more senses than one, if you understand my meaning. His name was Andrea Mattioli. Few Englishmen would have trusted him, but I knew that I could do so with safety. He had been born on my father's estate in Tuscany, and with we Italians the old feudal instinct is strong. I provided Mattioli with money and told him to frequent the low haunts of the underworld of London where I knew Boyd-Pennington occasionally sought relaxation. By pandering to his secret craving for drugs, Mattioli gradually wormed himself into the other's confidence, and one night, in a moment of half-stupefied boastfulness, Boyd-Pennington

let fall enough hints to enable me to guess the whole of the plan that he had in mind.

'It was a scheme such as I might have evolved myself if I had a desire to practise murder as a fine art.' The old man rubbed his hands and beamed like an ardent connoisseur who gloats over an artistic masterpiece. 'He did not intend just to kill Dorene Grey with his ingenious 'stabbing-gun' — if I may be permitted to coin a phrase. Oh, dear no! Nothing so crude and straightforward as that! He intended to kill another person altogether, under such damning circumstances that the law would do his dirty work for him by convicting and hanging the girl for the murder! I will not weary you by recounting the plot in detail. What happened in Rattenbury's office on the afternoon of the murder was all according to plan.

'Dorene was inveigled there by Mrs. Peters being bribed to bring the tempting advertisement to her notice. It was a stroke of good fortune — though not surprising — when Boyd-Pennington also

instructed Mrs. Peters to pass on the address and contact details of his good 'friend' Mattioli's London boarding house. On her arrival in London, the day before she planned to see Rattenbury, Dorene booked in with Mattioli. Naturally, he telephoned me immediately, and I knew that matters were moving to a head.

'Knowing Rattenbury's reputation, there was little fear of a third person being present at this interview with the pretty and inexperienced girl. Had Dorene actually been alone with him she would have no more seen the streak of the knife that killed him than you could distinguish a flying bullet on its path through the air. She would have been as puzzled as anyone to account for his death. As you know, she had already fled down the fire-ladder, but the very fact of her flight only seemed to make her guilt the more obvious. You yourself must admit that you would have tracked her down and arrested her had it not been for the dramatic confession of the Phantom of the Films. I was that Phantom, as you

know, and my friendship with Clifford Baxter gained me the access I needed. My sole object of making that film and inserting it into the spool that was to be shown at the Pantheon Theatre that night was to clear Dorene of the charge by my false confession.'

'But why was Mrs. Peters killed?'

'She knew too much,' was the swift answer. 'Her sphere of usefulness was past when she had drawn Miss Grey's attention to the advertisement that was to lure her to the agent's office. Only in this case the murderer's task was simplified to a quick shot from a car standing in the lane by the cottage garden.'

'Well, Professor, you certainly seem to have made a very thorough clean-up of all the loose ends of the mystery.' In spite of himself, the Assistant Commissioner could not help a note of admiration creeping into his voice. 'But still I can't understand why Julian Rotheimer should shield Miss Grey by allowing her to disguise herself as a programme-seller at his cinema on the night after the crime was committed.'

'That's simple enough. He told me that his brother was insured for a large sum, and the policy had a clause that barred suicide. Julian Rotheimer thought that his brother had killed himself — and, what is more, he thought that Dorene had seen him do it. He thought it good policy to keep her from telling her tale to the police, but when the Phantom confessed to the crime, he had no cause to fear anything she might tell.'

'As you know so much, Professor, maybe you know who ripped open the safe that night?' Sir Digby said.

'Certainly. It was the man whom you saw leaving the block in the car — Boyd-Pennington. He heard the Phantom's confession and knew it to be false. It must have come like a thunder-clap to him. He wondered who the mysterious apparition was, how much he knew, and what his motive was. He thought he could find out all these things by opening the safe, and he just managed to beat you to it. The only thing he found there was the contract which Dorene had signed before the murder, the contract

which I had so dramatically cancelled.'

There was a slight pause. Then Sir Digby, glancing through the window, uttered an exclamation.

'I think Miss Grey is not much the worse for her alarming experience,' he remarked with a smile. 'Look!'

The outlines of two figures were dimly visible in the window of the scenic set. The taller of the two was drawing the other's slender form towards him, bending his head until the upturned lips met his.

A wistful smile dawned on Professor Dangelli's wrinkled face and his keen eyes grew tender. But the next moment he burst into one of his sardonic chuckles as he thrust his head and shoulders out of the window and shouted across:

'Hold that picture! Hold it until I can get the cameras working again. Just — just as you look — you'll make the best possible final fade-out for the one and only drama produced by the Phantom of the Films!'

We do hope that you have enjoyed reading this large print book.

Did you know that all of our titles are available for purchase?

We publish a wide range of high quality large print books including:
**Romances, Mysteries, Classics
General Fiction
Non Fiction and Westerns**

Special interest titles available in large print are:
**The Little Oxford Dictionary
Music Book, Song Book
Hymn Book, Service Book**

Also available from us courtesy of Oxford University Press:
**Young Readers' Dictionary
(large print edition)
Young Readers' Thesaurus
(large print edition)**

For further information or a free brochure, please contact us at:
**Ulverscroft Large Print Books Ltd.,
The Green, Bradgate Road, Anstey,
Leicester, LE7 7FU, England.
Tel:** (00 44) **0116 236 4325
Fax:** (00 44) **0116 234 0205**

Other titles in the
Linford Mystery Library:

THE TOUCH OF HELL

Michael R. Linaker

The village of Shepthorne wasn't being gripped, but strangled by winter's blanket of snow and Arctic temperatures. The trouble began with a massive pile-up on frozen roads and a fireball of exploding petrol as a truck collided with a tanker in the garage forecourt. Then, from the sky, a huge military transport with its cargo of devastation crashed down towards the village. Hell was just beginning to touch Shepthorne . . .

SWEET SISTER DEATH

Frederick Nolan

The objective of PACT — a secret counter-terrorism organisation, is to eradicate the perpetrators of political assassination and terrorist acts, and Charles Garrett is their best weapon. A bizarre series of murders plunges Garrett into a deadly conspiracy mounted by the terrorist Leila Jarhoun — the leader of a suicide cell created to unleash a holocaust of death across Europe. Jarhoun always strikes where Garrett least expects, until finally she confronts him — three hundred and fifty feet above New York harbour . . .

THY ARM ALONE

John Russell Fearn

Betty Shapley was a local beauty, for whose charms three young men fell heavily. But her coquetry would lead to death for one of her admirers, Herbert Pollitt; a fugitive's life for another, Vincent Grey; and becoming a murder-case witness for the third, Tom Clayton. Inspector Morgan and Sergeant Claythorne investigate the death, and suspect Vincent Grey. So Betty, former pupil of Roseway College for Young Ladies, asks Miss Maria Black — 'Black Maria', the headmistress detective — to prove Grey's innocence.

MAN IN DUPLICATE

John Russell Fearn

Playboy millionaire Harvey Bradman is set an ultimatum by his fiancée: before she marries him, he must carry out some significant, courageous act. Amazingly, the next day the newspaper carries a full report of Harvey's heroic rescue of a woman from her stalled car on a level crossing, avoiding a rail crash! But Harvey had been asleep in bed at the time of the incident. And when his mysterious twin seeks him out, he becomes enmeshed in a sinister conspiracy . . .

FEAR OF STRANGERS

E. C. Tubb

Instead of the welcome they'd expected, the returning crew of the first interstellar spaceship were kept in space, imprisoned in their craft — in quarantine, as carriers of a deadly alien disease! When the prisoners escaped, the worried authorities hired Earth's top detective Martin Slade to track them down, little suspecting that Slade had his own personal agenda. Slade's search for the missing crew spans millions of miles of space, following a trail of hideous deaths . . .

KILL PETROSINO!

Frederick Nolan

It is the turn of the century. Lieutenant Joe Petrosino of the New York Police Department is a man with an obsession. Believing that there is a secret society controlling organised crime in America, he aims to expose the Mafia. With disbelieving superiors, he alone must face the feared Don Vito Cascio Ferro. Would-be informers are too scared to talk, but Petrosino gets his first lead with the discovery of a brutally murdered body in a New York alley . . .

D1344238